Pigeon-Blood Red

Pigeon-Blood Red

Ed Duncan

Acknowledgements

Thanks to my original editor, Karen S. Davis, and my later editor, Christopher Hassett, whose insightful comments and suggestions greatly improved this novel.

Thanks also to the folks at Voyage Media and Jacob Arden McClure, who designed an awesome front and back cover.

For Kristin, Anika, and Gregory

Part One

Chapter One

Jerry got out of the car, closed the door, and stretched. He bent down in front of the side-view mirror to check his hair. Satisfied, he straightened up and casually patted his right pants pocket.

Incredulous, he patted it again, and again. Then his left pocket. He did a quick search through his coat pockets.

"Shit," he said under his breath and flung open the car door with such force that it rocked back and forth on its hinges. Inside, he searched like somebody was holding a gun to his head and running out of patience. He rummaged between the seat cushions, under the seats, and under the floor mats on both sides of the car. Then he crawled between the front seats to the back and repeated the process.

Rico had gotten out of the car the same time Jerry did. By the time Jerry began his search, he had walked around to the passenger side and leaned against the car, arms folded across his chest. From there he watched the search, more bemused than concerned. When it was over he said simply, "He lifted it," and when Jerry pounded his fist on the roof and kicked a tire, "Get in."

They drove in silence, Jerry brooding and fidgeting the entire time. Rico looked over at him. "Relax."

But for the circumstances, it would have been a good day for a drive. It had rained the day before, but now the weather was crisp and clear, and the water that collected on the street and sidewalks glistened in the mid-day sun. With rush hour still hours away, they sailed through traffic.

Jerry looked around. They weren't heading in the direction of the racetrack, where they had dropped Robert McDuffie off forty-five minutes earlier. "I thought you said—"

"Jean's place is closer. I'll check her out while you take the car and check out the guy."

"But—"

"I'm ninety-nine point nine percent sure, but point one percent is still point one percent."

Jean lived in a venerable four-story apartment building tucked away in a well-preserved neighborhood on Chicago's southeast side a few minutes' drive from the lake. When Rico pressed the buzzer on the ground floor, she was taking a shower so she didn't hear it. He tried her cell and got voicemail. That was too bad because he couldn't wait. He had to go up. He hoped she was there and just didn't hear the buzzer because he liked her—no, he was crazy about her.

He didn't have a key to the main door, so he waited in the vestibule between the inner and outer door for someone to show up. It didn't take long.

A resident entered the building. He was in his mid-thirties, already balding, two inches taller than Rico and several pounds heavier, though the extra weight was more blubber than muscle. He had had a fight with his wife and was in a surly mood. To teach her a lesson he was making her carry all the groceries. She arrived thirty seconds after he did, huffing and puffing, while his breathing was as tranquil as a kitten's. He propped the outer door open with his foot and she struggled through with two heavy bags, brown paper with no handles, one in each arm like two large babies. Her husband had both hands free but didn't bother to help. After the door closed, he turned to Rico, who was facing the inner door.

He had said nothing to Rico all this time and Rico hadn't turned around to acknowledge him. He suspected that Rico intended to follow them into the building. He knew Rico didn't live there and didn't have a key. He didn't like the idea of letting him in—not because it was against the rules or because he thought Rico might be an unsavory character. He simply wasn't in the mood to be helpful.

Rico, a blank expression on his face, slowly turned and looked the man over from head to toe. The man glared contemptuously at Rico and turned his back to him while his wife, a plump woman with a round face and sparkling eyes, tried to keep the bags from falling by holding them up with one knee and then the other. Rico parted his lips to speak but before he could, the woman did.

"Henry, what's the matter with you?" Her impatient voice twanged like a guitar string. "Will you please open the door? Can't you see I'm about to drop these bags?"

"Shut up. There's a rule against letting strangers in the building," he barked, showing his bad teeth.

"Oh, Henry, don't be so unneighborly. Open the door, why don't you?"

"I said shut up."

"Will you at least help me put these bags down?"

"Put them down yourself."

Rico didn't generally lose his temper or get excited. Still more rarely did he take things personally. If something had to be done, he did it in a logical, methodical way with as little disruption as possible, and his personal satisfaction was irrelevant. But once in a while, mission and satisfaction coincided—like now.

Getting the door open was his objective. Making Henry open it was going to give him a great deal of satisfaction, and it wasn't even going to be disruptive.

Two sizeable steps put Rico directly in front of the woman, who by now was struggling mightily to put the bags on the floor without spilling their contents. He reached down and took one bag in each arm, then, as though they were filled with cotton balls, shifted them both to his left the moment Henry turned to confront him. He stared directly into Henry's eyes, saying nothing, a faint smile on his face.

That was all it took. Henry's body wilted and beads of perspiration sprouted on his forehead. He cleared his throat and almost gagged. He had swallowed his pride so quickly he almost choked on it. He hurriedly opened the door.

Not changing the expression on his face, Rico thrust the bags into Henry's chest and, holding the door open, motioned to the woman to go through first. Embarrassed, she thanked him and smiled self-consciously. He walked past her, barely acknowledging her gesture, then turned on his heel before climbing the three flights of stairs to Jean's apartment. He couldn't resist. He caught the man's eye and said, "Thanks, Henry."

When Rico knocked on Jean's door he was happy to hear the sound of footsteps. At least she was there. Maybe it was a good omen. Jean, a stunning redhead with a figure that made the heart leap, looked through the peephole, opened the door, and greeted him wrapped in a towel. She was even more tantalizing than she'd been in the car earlier that day. She wasn't completely dry, and here and there tiny droplets of water glistened on her arms and shoulders. Rico inhaled the subtle fragrance of her shower gel, but before it could distract him, a voice in his head reminded him, "Point one percent."

"I wasn't expecting you back so soon," she began, a playful, sultry smile on her face.

From the doorway Rico scanned the living room and saw nothing amiss. He walked in and closed the door behind him. *Too bad.* He only knew how to do this one way. "Jean, how long have you known me?" he asked stoically.

She was baffled. "You know as well as I do. What kind of a question is that?"

"I never tried to hide from you how I make my living, true?" They stood face to face, inches apart, before she took a few halting steps backward. "So you know what happens to people who don't tell me what I want to know, don't you?"

"Rico," she stammered, her voice trembling, "you aren't making any sense. What's this all about? I don't know what you're accusing me of, but I haven't done anything, I swear."

He took a straight razor from his coat pocket and opened it. As he walked toward her, she covered her face with her hands. He stepped behind her, thrust his left arm through the triangle formed by her hands pressing against her face, and grabbed her right shoulder. With his right hand he held the blunt side of the open razor against her right cheek.

"Where is it?"

"Please, Rico," she sobbed. "I don't know what you're talking about." He pressed harder and tightened his grip on her shoulder. "Please, please!"

"I don't believe you." He turned the sharp side to her cheek.

"Rico, not my face, please! I swear I don't know what you're talking about." Her tears puddled where the razor met her skin.

"Sorry, baby."

As Jean cried out he let the razor fall from his hand and, in one uninterrupted motion, expertly muzzled her scream with the same hand before the razor hit the floor. She fainted.

When she came to, she was lying on the couch where Rico had carried her. He stood with his back to her, talking to Jerry on the phone. Jerry hadn't been able to get past lobby security in Robert's building.

"He palmed it, right?" Jerry asked.

Rico glanced over his shoulder at Jean. "I'll be there in a few minutes." He hung up. "I had to be sure," he said unapologetically.

She shivered in her towel and glared at him, anger roiling in her eyes. He went to the bedroom and returned with a blanket, which she allowed him to drape around her shoulders.

"Sorry, baby. It was just business."

Still too furious to speak, she defiantly turned her back to him and silently dared him to say anything about it. A small victory but it was something. Ignoring the gesture, Rico walked out and closed the door softly behind him.

She was enraged, as much at herself as at him, because she knew that the next time he called she would answer. She tried to justify her emotions by telling herself that he'd stopped short of actually harming her and that he never would have. But who was she kidding? She could hope but she could never know for sure.

When the cab pulled up in front of Robert's building, Jerry was standing outside smoking a cigarette. It was an expensive high rise on the city's Gold Coast along Lake Michigan's north shore, with a security guard on duty twenty-four hours a day. There was no way around it; if they wanted to get into Robert's apartment, one way or another they'd have to deal with him. This was admittedly a minor detail, more of an annoyance than anything else.

Jerry knew Rico hated cigarette smoke. An icy stare from him whenever Jerry lit up was as effective a deterrent as a punch in the gut, so he put the fag out as Rico left the cab. Rico kept his body rock solid by lifting weights at a neighborhood gym, jogging regularly, and minimizing his intake of junk food. He didn't like the idea of second-hand smoke undoing any of his hard work.

"So what happened?" Jerry asked.

"She didn't have it."

"I could've told you that. She's good people."

"Don't start with me."

"But—"

"But nothing. Anybody can cross the line."

"Including me?" Jerry hoped Rico might exempt him but didn't expect it.

"Yeah, including you." The two men stared at each other for a long moment before Rico smiled. "No, not including you." The smile vanished as quickly as it had appeared and his eyes narrowed. "You know better."

The comment stung and Jerry hung his head a little, but it was true and he knew it. It wasn't easy to get close to Rico and not many people did. He was loyal to a fault, yet distant and brooding. Deadly as a cobra but with a dry, sometimes biting sense of humor. Brutally honest, he lacked guile. Hated hypocrisy. Loathed arrogance. If you were in a fight for your life against hopeless odds and could pick just one person to help even them out, he would be your choice every time. But if you needed a shoulder to cry on or even a pat on the back, you'd have to think long and hard before you settled on Rico.

"Now, about this guy…" Rico said, ignoring Jerry's reaction.

Jerry snapped out of it. "You have to tell the security guard who you want to see. He rings the apartment. If the person answers, the guard buzzes you in."

"High-class joint."

"No wonder he's always out of money."

"How much traffic in and out?"

"Not too bad so far."

Taking in as many details as his eyes could process in one sweep of the area, Rico slowly turned in a circle, looking for anything out of the ordinary, anything that counseled against getting on with the business at hand. Outside, there were pedestrians and cars passing everywhere, but it was a busy street, so there was nothing unusual about that. Inside, the foyer was empty except for the security guard. Nothing looked menacing. Nothing looked out of place. He nodded. "Okay?" Jerry nodded back. "Let's go and talk to the man."

They walked briskly to the entrance, donning sunglasses almost in unison, then glanced behind them one last time before opening the door. Rico nodded to a spot inside. Jerry planted himself there. Without slowing, Rico continued toward an oak-paneled counter facing the door, behind which sat an unarmed security guard casually reading a newspaper. He was about forty, with a gaunt face and stringy hair reaching below his collar. He was the kind of guy who went through life trying to keep from stepping on anyone's toes and hoping everyone would try to avoid stepping on his. He looked up in time to see Rico, advancing quickly in his direction, throw open his coat and jerk a .45 out of a powder-blue shoulder holster. He leapt to his feet and raised his hands above his head. Rico slammed the gun on the counter.

"Put 'em down," Rico said. Eyes bulging and hands shaking, the guard complied and his face took on the look of a condemned man who had just received word of a reprieve. "That's right. Relax," Rico said. "Now buzz Robert McDuffie's apartment." There was no answer. "Try again." Still no answer. "Get the key and take me up there," he ordered, then nodded in the direction of the .45 resting on the counter under his hand. "This'll be pointed at the back of your head on the way. Any questions?" The guard shook his head. "Then let's go."

The guard got the key from under the counter. Holstering the .45 along the way, Rico followed him to a glass door that led to a bank of elevators. The guard inserted the master key card and they walked through. He pressed "up" and they waited, Rico standing behind him. When the elevator arrived, a woman got off and they got on.

The elevator had floor-to-ceiling mirrors on three sides, allowing the guard to steal a furtive glance at Rico, who noticed.

"Okay, I lied. The gun is not pointed at the back of your head. Any objection?"

The guard shook his head and screwed his eyes shut. The elevator reached the tenth floor. At Robert's apartment Rico stepped to one side and, with a nod, signaled for the guard to knock. There was no answer.

"Open it," Rico said.

The guard unlocked the door. Rico glanced behind him and nodded to the guard to go in. He pressed the gun against his back and followed him, closing the door behind them. No lights were on and it was clear that the place was empty. Rico flipped a wall switch and two lamps bathed the living room in light. "Nice place," he mused. And it was. Off the expansive, tastefully furnished living room, with burnished hardwood floors and elegant artwork adorning the walls, was an equally elegant dining room, with a dazzling chandelier, matching antique table, buffet, and china cabinet. The modern kitchen had stylish stainless-steel appliances, teak cabinetry, granite countertops, and marble floors. On one side of the kitchen was a bedroom and on the other a traditional library with mahogany-paneled walls and a wood-burning fireplace. Beyond the library was the master bedroom. Rico made his way there, guard in tow.

He waved the guard to the far side of the room, then surveyed the inside of a capacious walk-in closet from top to bottom, visually inventorying its contents, and rummaged through a dresser. He spied a small black book on a nightstand by the king-size bed. After flipping through the pages, he slipped it in his pocket.

He knelt to look under the bed where he found a duffel bag stuffed with gym clothes. As he pulled it toward him a photo tumbled out, which he scanned and pocketed. Keeping an eye on the security guard, he stepped into the master bathroom far enough to get a good look at the contents of the medicine cabinet behind the mirror and inside the drawers of the cabinet under the double sink.

"Let's go," he said tersely to the guard. He suspected that his search of the bedroom and adjoining bathroom had yielded as much useful information as the apartment had to offer, but to make sure, keeping the guard in sight, he made a quick check of the other rooms and found nothing.

At the elevator Rico opened his coat just enough for the guard to see the butt of the holstered .45. "I won't point this at the back of your head going down either, but you know where it is."

The doors opened to reveal two men and a woman. The security guard entered first and Rico stood behind him. The elevator didn't stop again until it reached the lobby. The three passengers left the building and Rico followed the guard to the counter, where Jerry joined them.

"Well?" Rico asked.

"One guy came in. I told him the guard had stepped out for a few minutes and he said he'd come back."

Rico started toward the door, then pivoted to face the guard. "By the way, nice talking to you." The guard was still terrified but managed an uneasy smile. Rico turned and smiled to himself. When he and Jerry were safely out of the building, the guard wiped his brow with the back of his hand and immediately braced himself against the counter to prevent his legs from collapsing beneath him.

As they approached the car, Jerry said, "What do you think?" Rico shrugged. "I think we got a problem."

Chapter Two

Earlier That Day

The Hawthorne Race Course in Cicero is about twenty minutes from downtown Chicago. Robert McDuffie, a proud member of the black upper middle class, was there for at least a few hours on most days during the racing season, and he always sat in the same section, so he wasn't hard to spot when Rico and Jerry came looking for him. As the horses entered the clubhouse turn, Rico and Jerry approached him from behind, and before he knew they were there, Rico tapped him on the shoulder and said, "Let's go." Robert didn't bother to ask why. He knew. And he was pretty sure they didn't care whether he saw the end of the race or not. So without a peep, he stood and walked with them to their car like a puppy on a leash.

When they got there, Robert said, "What about my car?"

"It's not going anywhere," Rico said.

Robert shrugged and they all got in. Their destination was an unassuming ten-story office building a few blocks south of the Loop. Constructed of stone and brick that would have taken an earthquake to dislodge, it was a rock-solid edifice worthy of a place known as the city with broad shoulders. The men rode there in silence while they listened to jazz on the car radio. Robert tried to convince himself that, despite the personal escort, there was no reason to panic, so he closed his eyes and tried to stay calm. The music helped. Soothing sounds from Terence Blanchard's *Billie Holiday Songbook* filled the car, dampening his fear, and soon he had gone a long way toward persuading himself that everything would be all right.

They arrived at Frank Litvak's building twenty-five minutes later. His office was on the second floor and they took the stairs like always. It was good exercise. When Litvak saw Robert, he greeted him with a smile and a friendly pat on the back. With that gesture, Robert's remaining apprehension melted and he exhaled audibly. Litvak pretended not to notice and motioned him to have a seat in one of the two high-backed chairs facing Litvak's large, richly appointed mahogany desk that, except for its glass cover, was completely bare. Rico and Jerry relaxed on a polished leather couch behind Robert.

"So, what do you think of the Cubs' chances this year?" Litvak said after everyone sat down.

"I don't know. I'm more of a Sox fan," Robert said, only a tad self-consciously.

"I can see how you might be," Litvak said. "The Cubs suck. Always have." Then, without warning, Litvak's mood changed. He leaned forward and his voice dropped several octaves. "Where's the rest of my money?"

"Frank, you know I'm good for it and—"

"Bullshit. Where is it?" He held his meaty hands out, palms up, as though he were waiting for money to fall into them from above.

For the first time since Rico and Jerry scooped him up from the track, Robert started to sweat.

"I can get you five thousand this afternoon, but—"

"Five thousand, my ass," Litvak said. "You owe me almost fifty, and counting." He was a corpulent yet menacing man with a puffy face, a pink complexion, and an ever-expanding bald spot on the top of his head. He looked like somebody out of the pages of a wrestling magazine from a bygone era: a brawling street fighter who didn't mind drawing blood or kicking his opponent when he was down. Nearing fifty, he still exuded an air of intimidation, born of, ironically, a deep-seated insecurity, which demanded of his underlings both absolute loyalty and maximum obsequiousness.

"Come on, Frank. You got to give me a little time." In a matter of seconds Robert's armpits were soaked and beads of perspiration collected above his upper lip.

Litvak, as mercurial as he was menacing, rubbed his chin and thought for a moment. *What the hell.* Today was going to be a very good day. Under the circumstances, he could afford to be a little charitable. He leaned back in his chair and clasped his hands across his girth. "Perhaps I was being a little dramatic to make a point. Tell me, how much time do you need?"

Caught off guard, Robert, the man with the velvet tongue, tried to collect his thoughts but no words came. Litvak shrugged, raised his eyebrows, and curled his lips downward. "Well, I'm waiting."

"Give me a couple of weeks and I'll have everything I owe you."

Litvak leaned forward. "Seriously?"

He hadn't asked for an explanation but Robert knew he expected one. "I have a buyer for one of the stores...I turned them down, but I know I can get them back on board. They practically begged me to sell it to them."

"So why didn't you?"

"You know how much I love those stores. But if you aren't giving me any choice..."

Litvak was skeptical. "Which store is it?"

"The new one—my baby."

"How do they think they can make that store pay off when you can't?"

"Their pockets are a lot deeper than mine. Even with what I got from you, it was never enough to turn things around."

Robert lowered his head and rested his chin in his hands. He didn't have a buyer with deep pockets. He didn't even have one with shallow pockets. He had dug a hole for himself and Litvak was standing on his fingers as he tried to pull himself out.

Litvak heaved a great sigh. "How much time did you say?"

Robert lifted his head, hopeful. "Let me talk to them. I know they're still interested."

"I ask again. How long?"

"A couple of weeks, but..."

Litvak was smiling now. Robert had picked the time frame out of thin air, but Litvak intended to hang it around his neck, charitable mood or not. "But what?"

"It may take a little longer."

"You said two weeks."

"I know but—"

"But, nothing. Two weeks."

"Sure," Robert said and sweated a little more. "That sounds good."

Litvak stood and pointed to the empty anteroom. "Wait outside a minute while we attend to a little business."

When the door closed, Rico said, "By the way, where is Mickey?" Mickey was Litvak's bodyguard. He usually sat in the anteroom with Litvak's secretary, who was at lunch.

"He had a toothache, so I let him go to the dentist. Don't worry. I still know how to take care of myself."

Rico said, "Who's worried?"

Litvak stood. "Sometimes I wonder." He faced an oil painting that hung behind his desk. It was a reproduction of *Two Girls Lying on the Grass* by John Singer Sargent. Other paintings by lesser artists depicting assorted landscapes and still lifes hung on each of the remaining walls. The *Two Girls* was special, though, because Litvak's wife had bought it for him. But it was special for another reason: It covered an old-fashioned wall safe.

"I didn't know they still made those safes," Jerry said. But Rico knew and he knew the combination, too.

Litvak rotated the circular dial right, then left, then right again, opened the door, and extracted a pink velvet pouch. He loosened the string at the mouth, turned it over, and allowed its contents to slide into his palm: a necklace with sixteen color-matched rubies, each a prized pigeon-blood red. He held it up to the light from a window, marveled at it a moment, and carefully returned it to the pouch as though it were a delicate flower. He handed it to Rico. "You know what to do with this."

Rico slid it into his right front pants pocket, scarcely looking at it.

His given name was Richard but only a handful of people knew this. Growing up he had been called Rich until some Puerto Rican kids in his neighborhood translated that to Rico. He liked the sound of it and it stuck. Over the years it had become the only name he'd needed.

"Careful with that," Litvak said.

Rico raised an eyebrow but didn't say a word. He glanced at his watch and started for the door. Handsome in a sinister, foreboding way, he had an air of danger that seemed to attract women as much as his rugged good looks did. He was big and solidly built, well over six feet tall with dark sunken eyes, curly black hair, and a perpetual five o'clock shadow. Jerry, a little shorter and much more slender, got up to leave with him. He had a pale complexion, sandy brown hair, and wafer-thin lips. No matter the enterprise, he always tried harder than Rico because things never came as naturally to him as they did to Rico. Most of the time Jerry accepted this as a fact of life because dwelling on it only depressed him. He knew he wasn't the man Rico was or wanted him to be, and that wasn't going to change, no matter what he did. So why worry about it? Besides, he could take solace in knowing he wasn't alone. No one else could measure up to Rico either.

"Wait a minute." Litvak stopped them. "I almost forgot about our friend Bobby. Give him a ride back to his car." He yelled in the direction of the anteroom door. "Bobby, get in here."

Not certain what Litvak planned for him, Robert had stood near the door the whole time, his ear almost touching it, trying to decipher what was going on inside. He had heard Jerry's remark about the safe (although Jerry hadn't seen it before, Robert had) and Litvak's comment about being careful, so he surmised that Litvak had taken something out—probably something valuable—to be delivered somewhere. When he heard his name, he tiptoed back a few steps from the door before going in.

"Bobby, I'll see you in two weeks." Litvak ambled over and stood in front of him, a few feet separating them. His patronizing tone was almost fatherly. "Don't make me come looking for you, okay? I like you, kid. You remind me a little of myself before I smartened up." Robert flashed the smile Litvak expected but his stomach still churned.

"I thought I knew everything, too. I didn't and, trust me, you don't either. And now, you ask? Well, now is a different story, right guys?"

Rico and Jerry had been standing at the door patiently waiting for Litvak's lecture to end. Being the good soldier, Jerry looked at Robert and said, "You can take that to the bank."

Rico, meanwhile, made eye contact with Litvak and started out the door.

Jerry had felt obliged to deliver the affirmation Litvak's insecurity demanded, but Litvak still needed Rico's endorsement. He repeated, in a tone that didn't so much demand as plead, "Right, Rico?"

Rico paused and produced a smile that was barely there. "Anything you say."

Litvak frowned but the comment would have to do.

The three men quietly walked out to the stairs and down to the street. Rico turned up his collar against the March chill and handed the pouch to Jerry. "Take this. I'll drive."

Jerry looked puzzled but didn't object. He handed the key to Rico and deposited the pouch in his own front pants pocket. Robert reached for the back door.

"Hold on," Jerry said. "Get in front. If he's driving, I may as well stretch out."

"Don't get too comfortable back there," Rico said. "We gotta make a stop on the way."

Jerry shot him a look of worn exasperation but said nothing. He knew it would do no good.

Chapter Three

"Are you guys going to be long?" Robert asked after a few minutes. His wife Evelyn was leaving town with a friend for Honolulu in a few hours, and although they were barely speaking, he didn't want to make matters worse by not seeing her off.

"Don't worry," Jerry said. "This won't take long."

A half hour later they stopped in front of a four-story apartment building on South Paxton Avenue. The new owners had done an excellent job of rehabbing the place, which, befitting a neighborhood in the midst of gentrification, looked almost new while maintaining the patina of the original grand construction.

Rico went into the foyer and rang one of the apartments. Someone buzzed him in and he disappeared behind the inner door. A few minutes later he emerged with Jean. Her fiery red hair, blowing freely in the March wind, framed a nearly flawless oval face. While it hardly seemed necessary, it was obvious that she worked at looking good. She wore stiletto heels, a sheer white blouse, a black leather miniskirt, and a matching leather coat, long to her ankles.

As they approached the car, Jerry got out and greeted her by name. Jean smiled sweetly, like a fairytale princess, Robert thought, and she and Rico got in the back seat. Rico told Robert to keep his eyes facing forward. He obeyed but wondered what the hell was going on.

From time to time Rico had Jerry drove him and Jean around the city in the daylight—usually with an unsuspecting passenger in the front seat who was instructed not to turn around—while the couple came as close as possible to having sex without actually having it. This was one of the few expressions of Rico's freer spirit that rarely surfaced from below his otherwise gruff exterior. He got a kick out of people passing by and falling dumbstruck at the sight of him and Jean in any state of undress. Equally amusing was the plight of the front seat passenger, aware of what was happening behind him, dying to turn around yet unable to do so.

Jerry started to drive. "Eyes forward," he told Robert.

"Is anything wrong?" Robert asked.

"Just keep looking straight ahead."

Jerry drove on South Paxton until he reached the railroad tracks that ran parallel to East 71st Street. He crossed the tracks and took East 71st toward Lakeshore Drive. There were two lanes of travel in each direction on East 71st Street, and a car occupied by a middle-aged couple pulled alongside them when they stopped at a traffic light. The man in the passenger seat noticed first. His eyes widened and he leaned toward the window to get a better look. Then he tugged on the sleeve of the woman driving the car. She gasped and brought a hand to her mouth. Though visibly appalled, they couldn't help but hold their gaze, mouths agape, on the shameless indiscretion taking place in the car next to them.

Jerry slowly pulled away, enjoying the spectacle, and eventually turned north onto Lakeshore Drive, where the vehicle, and what was taking place within, continued to attract looks of disbelief from passing motorists or their passengers.

Robert, meanwhile, successfully resisted the urge to look. Once out of the corner of his eye he managed to glimpse Jean's perfectly contoured breasts, barely restrained by her black bra, which Rico worked methodically to free. When a portion of bare thigh flashed in the passenger side view mirror, he quickly turned his head and forced his eyes forward. Jerry looked over at him and smiled.

"What's the matter?" Jerry asked.

"Nothing," Robert said.

"No? It looked to me like you'd nearly snapped your neck a second ago, jerking your head around like that."

Robert nervously shifted positions in his seat. "Did I?"

Jerry looked at him with a sideways squint, let the air weigh heavy between them, then delivered his judgment. "You know what I think. I think you were looking back there." Jerry glanced at the rearview mirror, then flashed a menacing grin. "Yeah, you were taking a peek all right. Didn't I tell you not to do that?"

"I didn't," Robert said quickly, his shoulders suddenly stiff, his hands opened in a plea for mercy.

Again, Jerry feigned a weighted silence, a pause that had Robert twitching, blinking, shifting his head from side to side.

"Okay," he said, "I'll take your word for it. But don't let me catch you looking back there. Not even once." He checked the rearview mirror again and smiled. "And that includes me."

A few minutes later they were back in front of Jean's apartment building. She and Rico rearranged their clothes and got out of the car. Jean hadn't said a word the whole time. In that respect, Robert thought, she and Rico made a perfect couple. Jerry sent Robert to sit in the back seat and scooted over to the front passenger seat as Rico walked Jean to the door.

"What was that all about?" Robert asked.

"What do you mean?" Jerry said.

"Whatever was happening in the back seat."

"Oh, that. Listen, Rico has this thing. He gets a kick out of going at it with Jean in the back seat while I drive them around. Don't let it bother you."

"Going at it?"

"Getting close to doing something. But not quite."

"And you're okay with that?" Robert asked, genuinely appalled.

"I'm used to it," Jerry said. "Besides, they don't mind."

"Sounds sick to me."

Jerry laughed. "Sick? Where's your sense of humor?"

Robert sat back and felt something lodged in the crack between the cushions. He reached behind him and pulled it out. It was the pouch Litvak had entrusted to Rico. He slowly removed its contents. The snippets of conversation he'd heard now made sense. Litvak had removed this from his safe. It looked expensive. But how valuable was it? He looked up. Rico was heading back to the car. He returned the necklace to the pouch and slipped it into his sock.

When Rico opened the door, Jerry was still laughing. "You told him?" Rico asked.

Jerry cleared his throat and managed to restrain his laughter. "He said it sounded sick to him."

"Nobody's ever said that before," Rico said.

His tone was a little too serious for Robert. He quickly explained, "I didn't mean anything by it."

"Life's too short," Rico said. "She has a nice body, doesn't she?"

"I guess so," Robert said.

"You guess?" Jerry said.

"Then, yes," Robert said.

"She works hard to keep it that way," Rico said. "No reason to hide it." He turned to look at Robert. "Right?"

"No. No reason."

Rico turned back around and gave Jerry a wink. "Glad we straightened that out."

Robert was glad Rico was facing forward again. He couldn't concentrate with Rico looking at him. His mind raced. Was he being a complete idiot to even consider what he was contemplating? He knew he couldn't come up with the money he owed Litvak in two short weeks. He didn't want to think about what Litvak would do then. But he knew what Litvak would do if he actually stole the necklace.

Then there was the whole idea of taking something that didn't belong to him. He was a lot of things, but he wasn't a thief—yet. But was he really a thief if he stole from an unsavory character like Litvak, a loan shark and probably worse? He convinced himself that he was not.

Still, it was a gamble. But he was a gambler.

He had time to pack and make it to the airport. If Evelyn's plane wasn't full...How long would he be gone? He had no idea. Nor any idea what he would do with the contents of the pouch. But now wasn't the time to worry about it. He'd have time to think after the plane took off—assuming Rico and Jerry didn't kill him before he got to the airport. Until now he hadn't entertained that possibility, but suddenly he could focus on nothing else.

He stared at the bulge in his sock. It wasn't too late to put it back where he'd found it. They'd never know. He perspired heavily. The resolve he'd felt an instant earlier had melted away, and in its place was indecision rapidly morphing into panic. He froze and as he did, the car stopped in front of the racetrack. He didn't move.

"Get out of the car," Jerry said without looking back. Still Robert didn't budge. Jerry and Rico both turned around and stared at him. "Hey, you going deaf or something?" Jerry asked. "Get out of the car already."

The decision had been made for him. They looked right at him, close enough to touch him. He couldn't return the necklace now even if he wanted to. He could explain finding it in the back seat, but he couldn't explain how it got in his sock.

"I'm sorry," Robert said. "I don't know what I was thinking." He got out of the car and stood transfixed as it sped away. Robotically, he drove home and made his way to his apartment, locked the door behind him, and sank to the floor in a sitting position, his legs stretched outward and his back against the door. Staring at the ceiling like it wasn't there and clutching his chest with both hands, he inhaled deeply and tried in vain to slow the pace of his galloping heart.

Chapter Four

Their search of Robert's apartment having turned up nothing, Rico and Jerry went back to their car. Rico looked up and shaded his eyes from the sun. It had shone brightly earlier in the day, only to give way later to an angry dark sky, and now it peeked through the clouds and, aided by a gentle breeze, warmed the chilly March air. Jerry didn't notice. A chill gripped his body and he shivered as the image of the velvet pouch slipping from his pocket flashed across his mind for perhaps the tenth time.

Rico got behind the wheel. His search for clues to Robert's where-abouts had disclosed that luggage and toiletries were missing. Robert and his wife had gone somewhere. Maybe they were still in town, but his hunch was they had left the city. "I'll check the two stores. You take the college."

Jerry looked puzzled, so Rico added, "Where his wife works."

"I forgot. What's her name again?"

"Evelyn."

Jerry hesitated a moment. Then he said, "What about Frank?"

"What about him?" Rico said without a hint of emotion.

"We gotta break the news, don't we?" Jerry asked, squirming a little in his seat. This was going to be a rough meeting for him, but Rico didn't seem to empathize. "Yeah, we might as well take care of that now," was all he said.

They drove in silence. Jerry would have preferred telling Litvak over the phone, but Rico hadn't asked his opinion. He hoped Rico could think of something to make the telling easier. He caught himself reaching in his pocket for a cigarette.

Rico leaned back without looking at him. "A smoke isn't gonna help. Don't sweat it."

Litvak met them at his office door, angrily firing questions. "Where the hell've you been? Lou says you never made it to his place. Is he shittin' me? You left here hours ago!"

"Can we come in?" Rico asked evenly.

Litvak made an exaggerated, sweeping gesture with his arm. "Be my guest," he said. He sat at his desk, Rico and Jerry in the two chairs in front of it.

"We had a problem," Rico said.

"What kind of *problem?*"

Jerry summoned all the courage he could command, but his voice still shook. "The guy lifted it."

Litvak leaped to his feet, incredulous. "Whoa, whoa, whoa! He what?"

Jerry straightened his collar and shifted positions in his chair. He looked at Rico and decided to take his medicine. "While we were driving—"

"While we were driving, the pouch fell out of my pocket," Rico finished.

Jerry, both relieved and embarrassed, turned and stared out the window.

"It came out of my pocket and he got his hands on it before I knew it was gone."

"Are you serious?" Litvak almost screamed.

Rico wasn't sure whether the question was rhetorical, but he answered anyway. "Shit happens." Jerry looked at Rico, who gave him a comforting wink.

Litvak was beside himself. He stared at Rico through narrowed eyes. Finally, he sat down, took a deep breath, collected himself, and, in the

24

calmest voice he had used since they arrived, asked, "If you don't mind my asking, where the hell is he now?"

"We're working on that."

Litvak started to lose control again. "What are you telling me here? Where is he?"

"We're working on it."

"I heard you the first time," Litvak said, derisively enough to convince himself he was still in charge. He puffed himself up a bit more. "So if it's not asking too much, start at the beginning. Tell me what happened."

Rico told him, leaving out the part about handing the pouch off to Jerry, but including his escapade with Jean in the back seat of the car.

When he came to that part, Litvak mumbled, "Jesus Christ, Jesus Christ," and shook his head. "Are you positive she doesn't know anything?"

"If she knew, she'd've talked."

"You sure?"

"Positive."

"So you think he left town?"

"From what I saw in his apartment, that's what it looks like."

"Did you try his cell?"

"Why? Would you answer?"

Litvak glared.

"Let's say he answered," Rico said. "Let's say he didn't. Either way a call would spook him. I don't want him to know we know."

"He's not that stupid! He knows."

"He may *think* he knows, but he's not sure. Call him and he's sure. I say let him sweat."

"This is your problem. I don't care how you do it. Just get it back." He started to add, "or else," but decided it wasn't necessary—yet. It wasn't like Rico to be so careless. That bothered Litvak, but the truth was he would have been a lot more concerned if the necklace had slipped out of Jerry's pocket. Fortunately, Rico was the one who lost it, and because it was him, Litvak knew that he would do anything to get it back, even if it meant going to Timbuktu to do it. It was a matter of professional pride and he had that in spades.

Rico stood and Jerry followed suit. "Let's go. The man wants his property back."

Chapter Five

Ordinarily when Rico and Jerry worked together, they were a team. Rico did the talking—assuming talking was necessary—and Jerry stayed in the background to act as a lookout and to provide additional muscle in case of surprises. But sometimes circumstances dictated that they alter that routine. They had split up earlier that day because they knew one of two people had taken the necklace, and they needed to identify that person as soon as possible. It didn't take two people to pay a visit to either Robert or his wife because neither of them was going to put up a fight. The same logic applied to the task at hand, so Rico decided that Jerry would focus on Evelyn and he would focus on Robert. He broke the news to Jerry on the sidewalk outside Litvak's building.

Jerry was nervous. He could strong-arm a deadbeat with the best of them, but this was different. It required people skills he didn't have. He stood with both hands in his pants pockets, shoulders hunched forward, eyes sheepishly on the ground. "You sure you want me to handle this?"

"I wouldn't've asked you if I wasn't sure."

Jerry raised his eyes. "You know I'm not the best at this kind of thing."

"Yeah, I know."

He knew the answer to his next question but he asked it anyway. "This is a black lady, right?"

"Right."

"So won't it look funny—me coming in and asking about her, I mean?"

"Listen, I need you to do this," Rico said. "So suck it up."

"If you say so."

"I say so."

Rico dropped Jerry off at his car and Jerry went directly to the college where Evelyn worked. Even after Rico's pep talk, if you could call it a pep talk, he had still wanted to beg off. But after Rico took the fall for him with Litvak, he owed it to him to do his part to make things right. He just hoped he wouldn't screw things up and make matters worse, if that was possible.

Jerry steeled himself and walked into the main office as casually as possible. The administrative secretary, a pretty young black woman, sat behind a metal desk facing the door.

"Hi," Jerry said. "I wonder if you could help me."

"I'll try," the secretary said.

"I'm trying to locate one of your professors, Evelyn Rogers."

To Jerry's immense relief, the secretary didn't give him a second look. She entered Evelyn's name in the computer on her desk and pulled it up on her screen.

"Evelyn Rogers," she said, repeating the name to herself. She didn't ask for any additional information, but Jerry was so anxious that he volunteered more.

"I'm a friend of a friend visiting from out of town on business. I didn't call ahead of time because I wasn't sure about my schedule. But we finished early and I couldn't...I couldn't reach her at home or...or on her cell, so I thought I'd try her here since my meeting was just around the block."

With a couple of minor glitches, it came out just as he had rehearsed it twenty or thirty times during the drive there. It didn't matter that he hadn't stopped to catch his breath or that his explanation sounded like a mini-speech. The important thing was that he got it out. Now he just hoped she wouldn't ask him any follow-up questions, like what business he was in, the name of his company, or how his friend came to know Evelyn, because, with that speech, his mind had reached its capacity to memorize, and he doubted that he could ad lib.

He was lucky. The secretary was new in her position. Friendly and garrulous, she'd never heard the expression "loose lips sink ships" or any contemporary analogue thereof.

"So how do you like our fair city, Mr....?"

"Uh, Jones."

"How do you like our city, Mr. Jones?"

"Oh, I like it a lot."

"Where are you from, Mr. Jones?"

"Uh, Philadelphia."

"I really like Philadelphia. I have relatives there. You don't know any Hendersons, do you?"

"No, I don't."

"What part of town do you live in?"

Shit, Jerry said to himself. He had never been to Philadelphia and knew nothing about its neighborhoods.

"Well..." he began.

"Oh, listen to me, going on and on and wasting your time. Evelyn is out for a week, and...Come to think of it, somebody told me she was going to Honolulu for a second honeymoon. I'm sure she'll be upset that she missed you. But I know she'd rather be in Honolulu, wouldn't you?"

"I sure would," Jerry said with a sigh.

"I'm sorry I don't know what hotel she's staying at. Should I leave a note for her that you stopped by?"

"No, don't bother. I'll see her next time, but thanks anyway." Ecstatic, he left the building humming. *That wasn't so bad.* He had to resist the urge to jump in the air and click his heels together. When he called Rico on his cell, he hoped for a pat on the back, but he didn't expect it and Rico didn't surprise him.

"We can't wait a week. Let me see what I can find out on this end." Rico had a longer drive and had just arrived at Robert's original store.

He sat in his car not yet sure what he'd say. After a couple of minutes, he went in and asked for the manager.

"Hi. Walt Montgomery." Rico extended his hand.

The manager, a middle-aged black man, shook it and smiled. "Hello. Sylvester Littlefield. How can I help you?"

"I'm an old friend of Robert's." No reaction. Did the manager know anything about Robert's childhood? Rico didn't. *What if he grew up in an all-black neighborhood and this guy knows it? He probably knows less about Evelyn's background than Robert's.* He took a chance. "And Evelyn, too. She and I were kids together. I'm sure Robert never mentioned me. Till a few days ago I hadn't talked to either of them in years."

"I see," Littlefield said, somewhat skeptically.

Not great, but okay. "I bumped into Evelyn downtown a few days ago and she mentioned the second honeymoon in Honolulu. Boy, she and Robert are gonna love it over there."

"A few days ago? I guess she knows him better than he knows himself. He just decided to go today."

Shit! That was close. "Well, you know how he is. She told me she was going to have to work on him."

Littlefield let his guard down a little. "Well, she succeeded."

"Listen, she mentioned the name of the hotel and I forgot it just like that."

"Why don't you call him on his cell?"

"Truth is, by a strange coincidence I have to fly there today and I want to surprise them. Of course, I wouldn't want to horn in on the honeymoon. Maybe lunch or something."

Littlefield hesitated. "Quite a coincidence, all right—Honolulu, I mean."

"Yeah, my company does a lot of business there."

"And what kind of business would that be?"

Rico didn't miss a beat. "Import/export." He smiled confidently.

"I see." The manager looked uncertain.

Rico wondered whether he'd laid it on too thick. He casually looked around to see how many people were in the store. One customer and two other employees. This wasn't the kind of situation where you took a guy out or even roughed him up unless you had to. Littlefield was a minor player in this drama. Rico didn't have to go through him to get to Robert. That would create a lot of complications he didn't need, including tipping Robert off. Going around him made more sense. It'd be tricky but not impossible. He'd have to use his head rather than his .45, which he preferred. *Let's try it again.* He turned back to Littlefield and renewed his smile.

"Excuse me," Littlefield said unexpectedly. "What did you say your name was again?"

"Walt. Walt Montgomery."

He said he and Evelyn knew each other as kids, Littlefield thought, *and he knows about the store and the second honeymoon, so he's not a perfect stranger. Still, something seems a little out of place but I can't put my finger on it. Of course, I could call Robert, but that'd spoil this guy's surprise.*

He already knows they're in Honolulu. What possible harm could come from telling him the name of the hotel? He had to make a command decision.

"Mr. Montgomery, follow me and I'll give you the number and the name of the hotel."

"Thanks a lot," Rico said. "And remember. If you talk to him before I do—"

"Not a word. And tell him not to worry. I'll hold down the fort."

"I sure will."

Chapter Six

After touching base with Litvak, Rico checked on flights to Honolulu. There were two that afternoon. He decided to take the later one so he could spend a couple of hours with Jean. It never occurred to him that she might not let him in. Sure, she might be a little reluctant, but in the end, she would come around.

First, he went to his apartment and packed clothes for a few days. When he got to Jean's building, some kids were leaving and he managed to catch the inner door. *I wonder where Henry is?* he thought, smiling slyly as it shut behind him.

At Jean's door he raised his fist to knock, but heard voices inside. *Should've called.* He turned to walk away but stopped himself. "What the hell." He knocked. Jean saw him through the peephole and opened the door halfway. She wore an oversized T-shirt and nothing else.

"Can I come in?" He shifted his gaze up and down to the areas on the T-shirt that would have covered her undergarments, if she had been wearing any.

"I'm kinda busy right now," she replied, barely a decibel above a whisper.

Rico wondered whether she was still upset. "I should've called, but I'm leaving town in a couple of hours and I thought—"

"Who is it?" a man's voice bellowed from the bedroom. It sounded like someone in a big hurry and anxious to get started.

"Just a guy," she answered quickly. "He's leaving." She tried to hide the edge to her voice. Her eyes pleaded with Rico to leave.

The anxiety in her eyes didn't immediately register. Rico sighed heavily, disappointed but not angry. *At least she didn't bring up the razor.* He'd taken a chance by not calling. If she was busy with a client, so be it. It was just rotten luck. But you couldn't blame a guy for trying. A wink and a smile let her know he understood.

He turned to leave again but the voice from the bedroom, angry and insistent, stopped him cold. "I thought you said he was leaving."

She turned her head toward it to answer. "He is," she called. She had successfully masked the edge in her voice, but it was replaced by a plaintive tone that worried Rico. She smiled sadly at him. "Thanks," she said softly. "I'll see you when you get back, okay?"

Rico didn't get a chance to answer.

"If he's leaving, tell him to hurry the fuck up before I kick *his* ass—*and* yours."

Rico tightened his jaw. Jean knew what his expression meant. "Forget it. It's all talk," she said.

He knew how he felt and doubted anything she could say could change his mind, but he asked anyway. "Are you sure you're okay with this?"

"Yes, I'm sure. Really."

But the man continued his rant. "Don't make me come in there!"

Rico opened the door, causing Jean to take a step back. He leaned and whispered in her ear, "Maybe I better make sure."

She didn't bother trying to dissuade him. She closed her eyes, lowered her head, and slowly shook it resignedly from side to side, then slumped wearily onto the sofa. Rico closed the door behind him hard enough for the sound to travel to the bedroom, where the man jumped out of bed and pulled his pants on. Bare-chested, he marched into the living room. When he was about ten feet from Rico, Rico stopped his advance with a wave of his hand.

In his early thirties, a few years younger than Rico, the man had a rapidly receding hairline and a ruddy complexion. He stood about five feet ten, was well built, and weighed maybe two hundred and fifty pounds. And he looked like he knew his way around. Rico was taller and a few pounds lighter, but his physique, while not as massive, was no less impressive.

"What's your name, big man?"

He glowered at Rico, nostrils flaring. "Who the fuck are you to ask me who I am?"

"Her priest." The words came out neutral, almost friendly.

"Kiss my ass!"

Rico glanced at Jean, who had closed her eyes and turned off her emotions, dreading the worst. "Jean, what's his name?"

She opened her eyes as though awakening from a slumber, but the man broke in, spitting his words out. "Hey, smart ass, talk to me, not her." He thumped his index finger against his chest.

"Okay, I will. But you don't seem to want to answer a simple question."

"What the fuck do you care what my name is?"

True to his philosophy, Rico had tried to defuse the situation. But that hadn't worked and clearly only one thing would. He advanced to within arm's length of the man, who stood his ground. "I don't care really. But I like to know a man's name before I put my foot up his ass. Christ, we could be cousins." Rico smiled faintly, satisfied that he'd pushed the right button.

The man's eyes opened wide. "You lousy motherfucker," he said between clinched teeth as he reached for a .38 he had tucked in his waistband behind him. Before he could extract it, Rico grasped the man's arm, pinning it behind him, and spun him around. He anchored his right forearm under the man's chin, and with his left hand he forced the man's right arm up until the gun dropped to the floor. Struggling in vain to free himself, the man grimaced and grunted. Rico thrust the arm upward until he fractured first his elbow and then his shoulder. The man shrieked in pain. Hearing the bones crack, Jean covered her face in her hands.

Rico released his arm, which hung lifelessly from his shoulder. "Are we done?" he asked impassively. What if the man said yes? Although he had offered him a truce, it didn't make sense for him to leave there alive.

It didn't matter. The man twisted his head around as far as he could and spat. "Kiss my ass, *mister* motherfucker. You think this is over?"

Rico sighed. Propping him up to prevent him from collapsing, he jammed his left forearm under the man's chin and took hold of his own right biceps with his left hand. He quickly wrapped his right hand around the back of the man's head, forced it down hard toward his chest. The man lifted his good arm and tried in vain to free Rico's grip. Then he squatted and thrust his hips into Rico's midsection, but Rico relaxed his body and shifted backward, absorbing the force of the movement while maintaining his hold on the man's neck and head. Next Rico jerked the man's body upward and backward so that only his heels touched the floor. He tightened his grip and held the man's chin against his own forearm until, a few seconds later, the man stopped struggling. His legs went limp, his arms dangled lifelessly at his sides, and his breathing ceased.

Rico released his grip, stepped back, and let the man's body crumple to the floor. Then he strode to the bathroom and washed his hands.

"What was his name?" Rico asked, reentering the room.

"Is that all you have to say?" Jean asked, horrified. Her arms were wrapped around her knees, which she'd drawn up to her chest.

"For starters," he replied, a little surprised she was so upset, "if you don't know who a man is, you can't protect yourself."

"Protect yourself? He's dead," she said angrily.

"I'll let you figure that one out." He bent over the body and removed the man's wallet from his back pocket. He made a mental picture of the driver's license and leafed through the rest of the contents. He had a little over a thousand dollars in hundreds, fifties, and twenties.

Jean was still shaken. "Why did you have to kill him?" She started to cry.

To him it was a rhetorical question. He opened the wallet so she could see the cash from where she sat on the other side of the room. "Any of this belong to you?"

She didn't answer. He dropped the wallet and strolled over to stand in front of her. He explained in a measured cadence the way a teacher might to a class having difficulty with a concept he'd explained a dozen times before. "He tried to cap me a minute ago because he was in a hurry. No way did he deserve to leave here in one piece. But I gave him a shot. He didn't take it."

"I don't care. You didn't have to—"

"Yes, I did, sweetheart." The uncharacteristically hard edge in his voice startled her. She straightened up and stared at him. Having achieved the desired effect, Rico dialed it back a notch. "I didn't need to be looking over my shoulder every day, waiting for him to show up and take another crack at me. I already have enough reasons to watch my back because of shit I can't control. Him I could control."

She wiped away her tears, loath to admit that she could see his point of view, but the idea ultimately overcame the horror and pity that had fought against it. His world was full of violent people, and he survived by knowing how to navigate it. Moreover, he was as violent as the people around him, violent enough to have come close to slashing her face with a razor. How close she'd never know. By now she'd almost convinced herself he wouldn't have done it, but if she was so sure, why, she wondered, had she fainted?

The truth was that she could never be absolutely certain what was in Rico's mind. Yet, as a flower is drawn to the sun, she was drawn to him by a force she could neither explain nor control. Perhaps more importantly she knew that, in his own way, he was drawn to her as strongly as she was to him. Of that she was certain. How else could she justify her fealty to him, he who dismissed as "just business" an accusation that she was a common thief and, for good measure, threatened to mutilate her?

When she looked at Rico, he thought he read the look of quiet resignation in her eyes perfectly. He smiled and slyly glanced toward the bedroom. "Like I said, I'm leaving town for a few days and I thought—"

"No!" She felt repulsed.

"Why not?" he answered, genuinely surprised.

"Because it's sick. There's a dead man here, not even cold. Ten minutes ago he was in the same bed you want to take me to now. I don't even know if I can live here now."

He looked embarrassed. *Can't blame a guy for trying.* "You win. I'll call Jerry and have some people come over and get rid of this stiff. You want to take a ride with me till they finish?"

She looked at him with renewed astonishment.

"No, not that. Just a ride."

She nodded.

"On second thought, maybe we'll walk. Why don't you put something on while I call? Who *was* that guy, anyway?"

"Nobody," she said glumly and went into the bedroom to change.

They took a short walk while Jerry and two other men stuffed the body in a huge trunk, carried it out of the building, and loaded it into a van. When Rico and Jean returned, Jerry met them on the sidewalk outside the building. The other two men were in the van. Jerry pulled Rico aside.

"Can I borrow a C-note? I'm a little short and I got to make a run in a little while."

Rico reached in his pocket for a roll of bills and peeled two off. "Two fifties okay?"

When Jerry nodded and held out his hand, Rico noticed the ring on his middle finger, too big even for that one. The huge diamond setting made it look even bigger. Jerry rapidly thrust the money and his hand in his pocket.

"That ring looks familiar," Rico said casually.

"I took it off the stiff. You left it, so I didn't think you'd mind."

"I left it for a reason."

"Damn it, Rico. That ring has got to be worth nine or ten grand."

"You think I don't know that?"

"Yeah, but goddamn it. I hate to dump that kinda money in the river. It don't make sense."

"Get rid of it, Jerry. It's not worth it."

"Okay. I want to impress a lady friend of mine. After that, it's history. Scout's honor."

Jerry was always trying to impress someone. His father was a football fanatic, which worked out well for Jerry's three older brothers but not so well for him. His brothers all played football in high school and went to college on athletic scholarships. Jerry was no runt, but he lacked the size and agility of his brothers. While his father was cheering them on, Jerry was getting himself kicked out of school over and over for fighting. A psychologist would have called it overcompensation, but his father was not impressed, and throughout Jerry's teenage years, the distance between them grew ever wider. He died when Jerry was nineteen.

Jerry's mother was not so distant, but she was incapable of grasping the connection between his rebelliousness and his rocky relationship with his father. She couldn't fill the hole her husband had created, because she didn't even know it existed. But Jerry still tried to impress her, showering her with gifts she knew were the fruit of his criminal activities—gifts she stored in the closet or the basement unless she knew he was coming to visit.

Jerry knew what his mother was doing, but he kept on trying to impress her, the same way he tried to impress girlfriends and people like Rico and Litvak.

Chapter Seven

Evelyn McDuffie was an only child whose strict African American parents, both architects, poured their dreams into her and insisted she get an "A"—in every subject and in every endeavor. That required discipline and rules, many of which she chafed at but quietly followed throughout high school. By the time she started college she was ready to break free, especially from the rule preventing her from dating boys of a certain type. The type Robert personified.

Robert was everything her parents had dreaded: the glib hustler with the polished veneer. Possessed of less-than-average looks and unimpressive intelligence, he more than compensated for these deficiencies with enormous charm, a sparkling personality, and an easy confidence that attracted women like picnics attract ants. Evelyn fell under his spell.

The first time he saw her she was riding her bike from the library to her dorm. Bikes were popular on campus, in part because students couldn't bring cars to school unless they could demonstrate a "legitimate need." Robert didn't buy a bike because he thought riding one around campus was beneath him. Always a hard worker, he already had a part-time job and another lined up for the summer, and he planned to get a car as soon as he could come up with an excuse that would qualify as a legitimate need.

Evelyn was riding in the street as Robert walked along the sidewalk in the same direction. He looked over his shoulder when he heard her approaching. He stopped and stared as she pedaled by, barely noticing him. It was a mild September day and she was wearing shorts, sandals, and a loosely fitting short-sleeved sweatshirt. Robert liked what he saw and immediately trotted after her.

"Hey, wait up," he shouted when he was a few yards behind her.

She coasted to a stop and turned to face him. "Is anything wrong?"

He smiled broadly. "No, I just need a lift."

She didn't return the smile. "What?"

He walked closer until he was standing next to her with only a few feet separating them. "I just thought that since we're going in the same direction and you're riding, and I'm walking, you might want to give me a ride."

"That's some line," she said, smiling now.

"It's not a line. I really mean it."

"Well, as you can see, there's no place for you to ride."

"Yes, there is. I'll sit in your seat and you can ride on the handlebars. I promise I won't ride over any pot holes."

"I don't think so," she said.

"Then I'll ride on the handlebars."

"You don't give up, do you?"

"Not when I really want something."

"And what do you want?"

"Let's start with your name." She told him and he told her his. Then he asked, "Why haven't I seen you before now?"

"Maybe you have and just didn't notice."

He took a step backward, folded his arms in front of him, shook his head, and gazed at her admiringly. "Uh, uh. You, I never would have forgotten."

That brought another smile to her face.

She had always been beautiful in an effortless way. She knew it but didn't flaunt it. Her honey-brown complexion was flawless, her body svelte, taut, and nearly perfectly proportioned. When she walked into a room, heads turned. She didn't invite the attention but accepted it naturally, like the change of seasons. She happened to be attractive, and attractive women produce predictable reactions—in men particularly, but in women as well. That was a mere fact of life, and that was the way she looked at it.

They married shortly after college and almost from the beginning they were on different wavelengths. She could have seen what was coming if she hadn't been so consumed with rebelling against her parents. They had met Robert and had talked to him at length on several occasions. He didn't impress them. First, he hadn't been a serious student. Second, while he was ambitious, he lacked discipline and focus. For instance, he let them know his chief goal in life was to make a lot of money, but he couldn't explain to them how he intended to do it. Finally, although they could point to no concrete evidence, both parents had the distinct impression that Robert fancied himself a ladies' man.

After they announced their engagement, Evelyn's mother tried to talk her out of the marriage.

"You don't know him the way I do, Mom," Evelyn protested.

"Evelyn, I wish you knew how many daughters told their mothers exactly what you're telling me now and regretted it later."

"Mom, I know you and Dad want him to be perfect just like you always wanted me to be perfect. Well, I'm sorry. He's not perfect and neither am I."

"Maybe we did push you a little harder than we should have. But I think you turned out okay, don't you?"

"I appreciate everything you and Dad did for me. But this is one decision you'll have to let me make for myself."

"Yes, you're right. It is your decision. I'm just sorry I can't change your mind."

"Mom, you'll see. Everything will work out fine, because Robert and I love each other and that's what's important."

"I wish that were enough. A lot of wives go into a marriage thinking they can change their husbands, but you'll find out it's much harder than you think."

Her mother was right. It was much harder than she thought.

For the first few years the couple's differences were masked, for the most part, by their hectic lives. Evelyn got her PhD and taught math at a local college in Chicago. Robert buckled down and used his charm to borrow more money than they could afford in order to buy a large appliance store.

He was busy with the store sometimes twelve to fourteen hours a day and constantly talked about expanding the business. He had become a solid member of the black middle class but wasn't content to remain there. Despite the challenges, he was determined to go further. It was difficult to keep good employees. When a salesperson quit or was fired Robert had to fill in until he found a replacement. Yet he couldn't wait to buy another store.

Evelyn had no interest whatsoever in acquiring more stores. She thought Robert had his hands full with one. They fought constantly, but eventually he prevailed and bought another, larger than the first.

Robert had always gambled, mostly at racetracks, but never so much that he had to borrow money to pay his losses. During one of his forays at the track he met Frank Litvak. Recognizing people who were drowning in debt and needed to borrow more to stay afloat was Litvak's business, and the racetrack, where he spent a lot of time anyway, was a good place to look. He had spotted Robert at the track quite a few times before he approached him. Robert was always well dressed, usually in a suit and tie, and looked the part of a successful businessman. When he lost, which was often, even a casual observer could tell. Sometimes he seemed paralyzed by a loss and for several minutes sat perfectly still, staring straight ahead into nothingness, more zombie than man. Other times he'd pound the armrests of his chair with the heels of his fists and curse to himself under his breath. After observing one such reaction, Litvak casually walked over and started a conversation.

"Mind if I sit?"

"Be my guest."

"Rough day?"

"You could say so."

Litvak extended his hand. "Frank Litvak." Robert shook Litvak's hand and introduced himself.

"I'm here a lot. Looks like you are, too," Litvak said.

"I like the ponies."

"So, Robert, mind if I ask what business you're in?"

"I own a couple of appliance stores."

"Business good?"

"I do all right. You?"

"I'm in the carpet cleaning business. And I have some other things on the side."

"Like what?"

"Well, one of them is lending people money when they're tapped out at the bank."

Robert's ears perked up but he answered casually. "No kidding."

Litvak didn't press. If Robert was interested, he'd take the bait. "You have any carpets that need cleaning?"

"No, mostly hardwood," Robert said.

Litvak handed Robert a card. "In case you know anybody who needs their carpets cleaned."

Robert looked at the card and turned it over. "It doesn't say anything about your other business."

"Like I said, I do that on the side, mostly for friends and people they recommend. That kind of thing."

"How much money are we talking?"

Bait taken. "How much do you need?"

"I didn't say I needed any. I'm just curious."

"Let's just say my carpet cleaning business is very successful, which gives me a lot of room to do these other things." Litvak stood. "You need anything, you come and see me."

At the peak of the housing crash brought on by the Wall Street speculators, credit dried up for even the most credit-worthy institutions. So it was no surprise that Robert had trouble getting a conventional loan to cover initial operating costs at the second store, as well as the unanticipated expenses at the original store brought on by the recession. He held on to Litvak's card for months before finally contacting him. Rather than cutting back on his gambling, or reducing unnecessary expenses at his stores, or simply waiting it out until the markets eased, he instead foolishly borrowed thousands of dollars from Litvak to bridge a gap in his financing. His supreme confidence got him into trouble. With mounting interest, the initial outlay had grown to over ninety thousand dollars. The original store was doing well. Once the second was up and running he was sure he could repay Litvak without difficulty, even taking into account the unconscionable interest rate. This was his rationale for not telling Evelyn in the beginning about Litvak's involvement.

In short order the second store became even more profitable than he'd predicted. Litvak received regular payments and just as regularly, in conversations with Evelyn, Robert complimented himself on his foresight. But the new store meant more time away from home and more pressure. As Robert became even busier, their differences—like Evelyn's desire to start a family and Robert's resistance to the idea—erupted into the open.

One night when Robert got home after a long day at the stores, Evelyn greeted him at the door with a glass of wine. "How was your day?"

"Hectic, but I love it. I really do. Things are finally turning around."

He sat on the sofa. She poured herself a glass of wine and sat beside him. "I'm glad," she said. "When do you think things will settle down?"

"I don't know. But I'm close."

"Can we talk?"

"Sure, what's on your mind?"

"Us. I know you've been busy at the stores—busier than usual—but it seems like you've been busier than anyone should have to be almost from the day we bought the first one. It's like your whole life is tied up in those stores. Meanwhile, we hardly see each other."

"I know it seems like that," Robert consoled, "but things will definitely change. It's just going to take a while, that's all. After that, it'll be smooth sailing. I promise."

"Robert, that's a familiar story," she said with sudden irritation.

"I don't know what you're getting so upset about. This is for both of us. I'm just asking for a little patience. Which I'd expect you to give me. Remember, you didn't think I could pull this off and I have."

In fact, Evelyn was impressed—and contrite. Robert had complained about her lack of support and faith in him, and now she had to acknowledge that he'd been right. Maybe, she thought, she'd been too hard on him in other ways. Yes, he was a dreamer, but sometimes dreams came true.

"And I'm happy for you," she conceded.

"Me? Just me?"

"Us then."

"See, that's what I mean."

"I said 'you' because I don't need all the extra money you're trying to accumulate. *We* don't need it."

"Then what about our family?"

"Are you just saying that to get me to stop complaining?"

"Of course not."

"You know we've talked about this before and you keep putting me off."

"I'm not putting you off now. I'm serious. I want a family just as much as you do. But I need you to wait until I get past this rough patch. We're almost there. I can feel it."

Evelyn didn't believe him but she let it go there.

And Robert kept on working late.

* * *

Then the bottom fell out. Big box stores, operated by national chains with limitless resources and deeply discounted prices, came in waves—first blanketing the community around Robert's new store, then the old one. Robert couldn't compete.

The pressure became enormous. He drank more than usual and more often. He wasn't a happy drunk and when he'd had too much, his frustration spilled out of him in an angry torrent of false bravado.

More than once in one bar or another he narrowly escaped getting his head handed to him because of some stupid comment bathed in liquor.

He also gambled more and more, and usually lost. Then he needed even more money, requiring more dealings with Litvak, who happily fed his habit. Before the crisis hit, he had reduced the ninety thousand he owed Litvak down to twenty. Now it had inched back up to fifty and he couldn't seem to keep it from going higher.

Until this juncture, Robert had been unfaithful only infrequently. He had never been a saint where other women were concerned, but he had managed to restrain his appetite. Now that changed, too.

Evelyn bit her tongue for as long as she could, but when she finally spoke, it was to give their marriage one last chance. Her friend Rachel Gatlin visited an exotic place almost every year because a relative in the travel industry got her discounted tickets. Evelyn had been trying to convince Robert to go for the last two years. Now she insisted. If there was any chance of putting some spark back in their relationship, this might do it. One day in September she called Rachel, got details about trips in March, and made the necessary reservations without clearing it with Robert.

When she discussed it with him, he resisted. He was still hoping against hope to turn the stores around. "Who would look after them?" he countered. It was a thin argument. He had a perfectly competent sales manager. And things couldn't get much worse in a single week. One day in mid-February, as they sat down to breakfast, matters came to a head.

"Robert, you still haven't said you're coming with me. Things can't go on like this much longer," Evelyn pleaded. "We need to get away and talk."

"Why can't we talk here?"

"We've tried to. We need a change. This can be like a second honeymoon."

"Okay. I'll think about it. But I need a few months to get things in order." He was trying to buy time, something that came natural to him.

"No!" she retorted. "You know I've already made reservations. We're going in March or I'm going alone. If you want this marriage to work, you have to stop thinking so much about those stores and start thinking about us. It's March or not at all."

That was the excuse he needed. He wouldn't be given an ultimatum. "Well, I guess it's not at all." Evelyn rose from the kitchen table, went to their bedroom, and started to pack. Robert looked on in amazement.

Their marriage limped along after that. Defiantly (uncharacteristically for her) she made good on her threat to go without him. When she asked Rachel to take his place her friend initially declined, protesting that she didn't want to get in the middle of a marital squabble. But after some cajoling, and Evelyn's promise not to cramp Rachel's style by acting like an old married lady, she was able to change her mind. Although her marriage was in ruins, Evelyn was in heaven.

Chapter Eight

Robert left the foyer of his apartment building, suitcase in hand, eyes searching in both directions for a cab. He had been lucky. He had gone online and booked one of the three remaining seats on the flight to Honolulu. He even found a room at the hotel where Evelyn was staying.

It was a slow day for cabs. Usually he waited a minute or two. After five minutes he got nervous. He was about to call on his cell when one pulled up. He got in, settled back in the seat, and closed his eyes. The feeling of relief washing over him was almost surreal, and for the first time since the necklace found its way into his grasp, he relaxed.

A mere four minutes after the taxi departed, Jerry showed up at the apartment building, missing his prey by the slimmest of margins.

While he hastily packed, he phoned his head store manager and talked longer than he wanted to. After that he didn't dare spend one minute more in the apartment than necessary. He planned to call Evelyn from the taxi as soon as his head cleared.

Now the old juices started flowing and he concocted the broad outlines of a story in moments. The truth was that until that instant he still hadn't figured out what to do or what to tell Evelyn. She was sitting in the boarding area talking to Rachel when he punched in her number. When she answered, he preempted the question he knew she would ask.

"I know you're wondering why I'm calling now, when I didn't bother to show up to see you off, but please hear me out because I have a good reason." She said nothing, so he continued. "Actually, I have two reasons; that is, I have two surprises for you."

"Get to the point, Robert," she said icily.

"Give me a chance to explain, okay? The first surprise is that I bought something for you—something you won't believe."

"Robert, as much as you need money right now, you shouldn't—"

"Don't worry. I won some money at the track. A lot of it."

"Are you kidding?" She sounded exasperated.

"Can't I buy something nice for my wife if I want to?"

"I give up."

"Don't you want to hear about the second surprise?" She sighed. "Such enthusiasm! The second surprise is I'm on my way to the airport now. I'm coming with you."

"You're what?!"

"I said I'm coming with you. Don't you want me to? I mean, this was your idea and now you're upset with me after I pulled all these strings to get away and surprise you at the last minute. You know how tough things are at the stores now."

"Yes, I wanted you to come—six weeks ago or even two weeks ago. But now I've made other plans."

"Rachel is a good kid. She'll understand."

"Maybe she would, but why should she have to?"

"Fine. Be like that if you want to," he said in his best imitation of a rejected lover. "I have a seat on the plane and my own room at your hotel. I'll have to convince you I'm being straight with you."

"It's a free country," she said, and disconnected.

Evelyn hadn't bothered to disguise her conversation with Robert, and Rachel had been listening intently. As soon as Evelyn disconnected, she asked expectantly, "So, what's the deal?"

"He's invited himself along." Evelyn said the words robotically, as if she'd fallen into a trance. "He's on his way here now, and he has a room at the hotel."

"Would you like me to switch with him?"

Suddenly, Evelyn's anger returned. "No way," she snapped. "He can stay in his own damn room. Maybe that'll teach him a lesson."

"Slow down. I was trying to help."

"I'm sorry, Rachel. I don't mean to take it out on you. Sometimes, that man..."

"It's okay," Rachel said, putting her arm around Evelyn's shoulder. "We'll play it by ear."

Rachel and Evelyn were more than acquaintances but they weren't best friends, which was why Evelyn wasn't surprised when she had to coax Rachel into going in the first place. She had backed herself into a corner with Robert by insisting that she would make the trip with or without him, but she preferred not to go alone. None of her closer friends could get away, and Rachel knew the islands and had the right travel connections.

Evelyn had always viewed Rachel as a bit of an enigma. They met at the college where they both taught. Rachel was more gregarious. She dated a lot, and each time it seemed to be a different guy. Occasionally she would double date with Robert and Evelyn. Everyone got along well enough, but it always struck Evelyn that something about Rachel was hidden right below the surface, something that made it difficult to get to know her well.

She had a restlessness about her. She was constantly on the go and not nearly as dedicated to her job as Evelyn was. She had been working on a PhD in history for ages, but recently she'd confessed to Evelyn that she was merely going through the motions and never expected to finish it. For that matter she didn't expect to be at her current job much longer. Although she wasn't sure what she was going to do, the uncertainty didn't seem to trouble her. It would have driven Evelyn to distraction.

Thinking about Robert now—the enormous disappointment he had become and the terrible angst he had brought to their lives—Evelyn wondered whether just maybe Rachel, and not she, had the right outlook on life.

Chapter Nine

The plane touched down in Honolulu without incident. Robert's seat was several rows behind his wife's, making it convenient for her not to speak to him. She didn't know it but that suited his plans, since he was still perfecting the pitch he'd deliver to her when they reached the hotel. When she passed him on the way to the bathroom she looked straight ahead, and he pretended to be asleep. They did share a taxi to the hotel, but the standoff between them continued, she talking to Rachel in the back seat and he engaging in small talk with the driver in front.

After they checked in, Robert got Rachel's attention with a raised eyebrow and an imploring gaze. Obligingly she cleared her throat and announced that she'd go ahead with their luggage and meet Evelyn in their room. Robert handed her a tip for the bellman, which she tried to decline, but he insisted and forced a bill into her hand with a smile.

The whole time, Evelyn stood by in stony silence, arms folded resolutely across her chest. When Rachel was out of earshot, Robert, in a voice bathed in self-pity, assumed the role of penitent husband seeking forgiveness and a second chance. "I know everything that's happened between us is my fault. But I intend to do whatever it takes to make things right." Unimpressed, Evelyn raised her eyebrows, sighed wearily, and looked away. "I know you're upset and you have a right to be, but all I'm asking is a chance to explain. If you don't like what I have to say, I'm on the next plane out of here, no questions asked.

But do me one favor. Don't say anything now. Sleep on it and let me explain tomorrow. Is that fair?"

*Fair? Really? So he wants to leave me in suspense until tomorrow. Well, if that's his game...*She faced him. "Robert, I don't know what you have in mind, but if you want to talk tomorrow, that's fine with me. Rachel and I have already made plans for part of the day but I'll call you when we're done." She ran to catch up with Rachel. In fact, they hadn't made any plans, but he could cool his heels until she was good and ready to talk to him.

Feigning gratitude, Robert called after her, "That sounds great." He was miffed by her coolness, but nothing in his voice or expression betrayed him.

The next day Evelyn and Rachel headed for Waikiki Beach. It was overrun by tourists, but still beautiful and exciting and lively and enticing. On the way, at one of the many shops lining their route, they bought straw mats to lie on under an umbrella on the sand. Once settled on the beach, they sat back and Evelyn removed a copy of *The Killer Angels* from her bag.

"Still a Civil War buff, huh?" Rachel asked.

"Can't seem to get enough."

"Funny, isn't it?"

"Because you're the history professor?"

"No, because you and Robert are having your own Civil War."

Evelyn set her book aside and looked out at the ocean. Rachel was right. For the past few weeks, she had engaged her husband as though they were ambassadors of enemy nations. When she said her wedding vows, she had looked forward to an enduring relationship based on love and mutual trust, but now she saw her marriage as a one-sided contract. But while it might not be pretty, and in some cases might even take a war, all contracts—be they treaties or marriages—could be undone.

She hated to admit that she had given up, but her mind had already made the raw calculation. Numbers and complex equations she could understand, but not Robert. He defied all logic. For better or for worse, she was finally convinced that he would eventually destroy his life. She had been bailing water for years, but his ship was finally sinking. She didn't intend to go down with him.

"I guess you're right," she said finally. "We are having our own Civil War."

"I was just kidding. Is it that bad?"

Evelyn took a deep breath and let it out slowly. Like a woman reluctantly coming to terms with the fact that she was never going to be able to shoehorn her feet into a pair of new high heels that were a couple of sizes too small, she had finally given up the struggle. "I think it's hopeless."

"Really?"

"All the time he spends at the stores. All the gambling and debts. And..."

"And what?"

"The women, of course."

"Are you serious?"

"He has a credit card he uses for the stores, but the statements used to come to our apartment and we'd deliver them to our accountant. A while ago I opened one by mistake and saw a few charges from some hotels in town."

"They could be business expenses of some kind, couldn't they?"

"I suppose they could have been, but they weren't."

"So you asked him?"

"He said he had paid hotel expenses for salespeople from out of town a few times, you know, as a way to develop business."

"That makes sense to me."

"It did to me, too, at first. But I was suspicious so I went to our accountant's office and asked to look at the business expenses over the last several months."

"Wasn't that awkward?"

"He knows I teach math. I told him I wanted to use them for a project for one of my classes."

"So what did you find?"

"Charges for flowers, jewelry, women's clothing. All kinds of things. Going back for months. And there were dozens of them."

"The nerve! Did you confront him?"

"I didn't have to. The statements suddenly started going directly to the accountant. He said he'd been meaning to make the change for a while and just got around to it."

"I would have thrown those statements right in his face."

"I know. That's the difference between you and me." Evelyn took another deep breath and exhaled slowly. "But it's finally over. I'm leaving him."

It hurt her to say those words. A part of her still cared for him, but whatever passion there had been between them had died like cooling embers on a cold winter night. Enough was enough.

"My God. I didn't know it was that bad. I'm sorry, Evelyn."

"Don't be. I'm glad it wasn't as obvious to everyone else as it was to me. But I'll work it out. And don't let it spoil your vacation. Which reminds me..." She turned on her side and faced Rachel for the first time. "Thanks again for coming. I know I had to twist your arm a little, but I'm glad you came."

Rachel reached over and put her hand on Evelyn's shoulder. "You know the song," she said and softly sang the words. "That's what friends are for..."

Evelyn smiled and wiped away a tear, then got to her feet. "Why don't we hit the surf?"

"Girl, and ruin my hair?" Rachel laughed.

"Girl, and ruin *my* hair?" Evelyn shot back. "I'm talking about some serious wading. All the way up to my knees!"

They both laughed and scampered toward the ocean.

* * *

Their foray into the ocean lasted all of fifteen minutes, during which they actually managed to get their bikini bottoms wet. Afterward, Evelyn and Rachel lay on the beach for almost three hours reading their books before Evelyn decided she had made Robert squirm enough. When she called, he was in his room waiting for his cell to ring. They decided to meet at one of the nearby hotels that had a restaurant with a patio abutting the beach. Rachel used the time to go shopping.

Evelyn waited on the beach outside the restaurant. As Robert approached, she noticed him looking over his shoulder. "Are you expecting someone?"

"No, why do you ask?" He was surprised it was that obvious. He was still terrified that Litvak's henchmen might sneak up behind him any minute.

"You kept looking behind you."

"Oh, that," he said. And the joke rolled off his tongue. He immediately wished he had thought of a different one. "There's an attractive woman who's been stalking me. I told her I'm married, but she wouldn't take no for an answer. I think I finally lost her."

Evelyn rolled her eyes. *Some ego.* They found a table facing the ocean and nursed tropical drinks. Evelyn had a Blue Hawaii and Robert a Tropical Itch. The turquoise waves rolled out to sea and back, carrying surfers perched precariously on their boards. Sun worshipers, old and young, fit and not so fit, promenaded from one end of the beach to the other. Here and there sea gulls glided above the waves, occasionally plunging into the water to spear a fish before taking flight again. Temporarily swayed by the idyllic setting, Evelyn felt her resistance wane ever so slightly. "I think I could stay here forever," she mused.

"Great view, huh?"

"Yes, fantastic." She let herself forget for a brief moment what a horrible mess her life had become.

"Then you're having fun?"

"Rachel and I are having a great time," she shot back, her resolve returning. She couldn't let her guard down now.

"You really know how to twist the knife, don't you?"

"Spare me," she said as though she were addressing a creature that just crawled out of the sewer.

"Okay, maybe I deserved that."

"Maybe? Please."

Robert shifted uncomfortably in his chair and took a long swig from his drink. This was going to be tougher than he thought. "Listen, I told you I hit it big at the track and I had a surprise for you. Well, the first thing I did was to go out and get something for you. I know things haven't been too great between us for a while and I wanted to try to make it up to you. I thought I'd have enough time to get back before you left for the airport, but of course I didn't make it." He waited for a positive reaction, but all he saw was a raised eyebrow and a dubious look. "Since you and Rachel were headed over here anyway, I thought I'd tag along and we could celebrate. I had to do some fancy footwork with the stores—"

"If you're telling the truth this time—"

"Evelyn—"

"If you're telling the truth, then...I'm happy you won some extra money and I'm happy you finally realize what's happened to our marriage, but it's a little late for an apology."

"I know what you're thinking, but all of that's in the past."

"Really, Robert? What part of it?"

"The whole thing. The gambling. The drinking. Staying out all night. All of it."

Evelyn shook her head cynically.

"What? Did I miss something?" he asked.

"Did you?"

Momentarily stymied, Robert decided to show her the necklace. He took the pouch out of his pocket, reached in and gingerly lifted it out. "I didn't even have time to get it gift-wrapped."

Evelyn was no expert, but she could tell immediately that it was an exquisite piece of jewelry. "It's beautiful," she said. "But..."

"But what?"

"You're so transparent. You're trying to buy me." She no longer hoped he wasn't. The wall she'd built around herself had crumbled. She no longer wanted to believe him, and she no longer wanted their marriage to work.

"I want you to have it, that's all. You deserve it after putting up with me for so long."

"Robert, you—"

"Do me a favor. Hang onto it while we're here. If you still want me to, I'll return it when we get back to Chicago, okay? Right now, I have to run. I'll call you later."

"No." She pushed the necklace back across the table, as he knew she would.

"Okay, have it your way." He slipped it back in the pouch and into his pocket. "I have to run, but I won't leave unless you promise me you'll wear it tonight." When he saw her look of surprise he said, "Unless you let me take you and Rachel to dinner, I won't have the pleasure of seeing how it looks on you, will I?"

Before she could answer, he'd already stood up and started to walk away.

Part Two

Chapter Ten

One Year Earlier

Paul Elliott's law firm occupied the entire thirty-second floor of a gleaming high-rise in downtown Chicago, and from his office he had an unobstructed view of Lake Michigan. He fixed his gaze on the lake and let his mind wander as he made the call. Although everyone in the office expected his trial would end that afternoon, they had no idea how long the jury would be out. So when Paul quietly slipped in and out, they assumed the jury hadn't reached a verdict and would resume deliberations on Monday.

But they were wrong. Paul lost.

The jury verdict came in on Friday afternoon, 4:30. Some judges let the lawyers talk to the jury afterward and some don't. This judge didn't, so Paul went directly to the office to drop off his trial bags and call his wife.

It had been a tough case and he didn't feel like talking about it. He hated lawyers who claimed they never lost a case. Either they hadn't tried many or they were liars—maybe both. Even if you think you have the best case in the world, you never really know until the jury comes back with the verdict. Juries are simply unpredictable. Even a great lawyer with a great case can't relax while the jury is still out. A great lawyer can still lose.

But Paul hadn't even had a great case. In fact, it was terrible. Bad facts. Bad law. *And* he had to defend an unlikeable client. Under those circumstances, even if your name is Clarence Darrow and the other lawyer is a bumbling idiot, chances are the result won't be pretty. That kind of case you try to settle. The problem is, if the other lawyer is any good, he probably knows he has you by the short hairs and the price goes up. (Or down if you represent the plaintiff.) If it's too high (or too low) you have to roll the dice and hope for the best. Every so often you get lucky, but most of the time you don't. Paul had rolled the dice. Knowing the odds hadn't made losing any easier. It never did.

Looking at him, you'd never have guessed the outcome. Both in and outside the courtroom, regardless of the true state of affairs, his motto was the same one every good trial lawyer tried to live by: "Never let them see you sweat."

After breaking the news to his wife over the phone in his customary low-key manner, he asked if she'd go jogging with him when he got home. She was tired and at first begged off. Then, sensing disquiet beneath his calm veneer, she acquiesced, as she usually did when, despite his best efforts to conceal it, she discerned something was important to him.

Paul opened the door and threw his briefcase and overcoat on the couch. He lived in a spacious three-bedroom apartment in a high rise in Hyde Park, an integrated community encompassing the sprawling University of Chicago campus that prided itself on being socially progressive and politically liberal. He felt guilty about having to coax his wife to come jogging, but he needed to blow off steam and wanted her along. She was a good runner and would press him to run at a good clip.

"JoAnne?"

No answer. He tiptoed to the bedroom where she lay casually across the bed, face up, fast asleep in gossamer baby blue panties and matching bra. Her jogging suit lay beside her. He gazed at her for a long moment and questioned whether jogging was still such a good idea.

She stirred. "Hi," she yawned. "Been here long?" She pointed her toes, tightening the muscles in her legs, and stretched her arms high above her head, accentuating the soft curves of her petite brown frame. She was even more desirable than when he'd entered the bedroom.

"Long enough. I'm just wondering whether I still want to go jogging."

"Up to you. It was your idea, remember?" She turned over onto her stomach, playfully bending one leg at the knee, and looked at him over her shoulder. "I'm a little tired, but..."

He drank in her shoulder-length dark hair, which complemented her mocha complexion, and her large, round, brown eyes that always reminded him of a puppy dog's. Her full lips were inviting as she lay there toying with him. He crossed his arms in front of his chest and loosened his tie, then breathed in deeply and slowly exhaled. "Don't tempt me," he said, not really meaning it.

"Am I doing that?"

"If we don't leave now, we never will. After a nice run, a hot shower, a little wine and soft music..."

"Are you sure?" she teased.

"Yeah, I'm sure," he said with mock firmness. He reached over and, with one finger, lifted the elastic waistband of her panties and released it with a gentle snap. Then he softly patted her behind.

"Save that thought," she said smiling, and scampered out of bed.

Five minutes later they were on the street jogging, a gentle breeze at their backs.

* * *

Wendell Broadnax was at the bar a mere forty-five minutes, but long enough to drink five gin and tonics. Now he was back in his car, weaving his way through traffic toward home.

"Why'd I ever marry that bitch?" he slurred. They had little in common and had done nothing but fight since they were married a month earlier. The truth was that she wondered the same thing about him—and with better reason. He'd started most of the arguments, including the one that afternoon. She complained about his constant drinking. Now he was giving her something she could really complain about.

He was thoroughly inebriated, but not too drunk to understand the drinks hadn't solved his problem. If something didn't change, he still had to face his wife for the rest of his life—or hers.

He continued driving, all the while slowly picking up speed. He changed radio stations.

* * *

Paul and JoAnne jogged at a steady pace. Earphone wires to their iPods hung loosely around their necks.

"You know you can't win them all," JoAnne consoled, wiping perspiration from her brow with the back of her hand.

"I know, but you always hope. You know why?"

"Tell me."

"Because sometimes you lose a case you know the worst lawyer in the world couldn't have lost, and the next time you win one you didn't have a snowball's chance in hell of winning."

"Sounds like a roller coaster."

"Not always."

"But often enough?"

"Yeah, often enough," he conceded. He considered elaborating and thought better of it. He hated to dwell on losses and he was trying to put this one behind him. "How was your day?"

"A lot better than yours." By day she was a bank loan officer, poring over documents, and at night and on weekends a frustrated writer of poetry and short stories. "But we did have a holdup," she said matter-of-factly.

"What?!" He grabbed her arm and brought them to a sudden stop.

"A holdup."

"Why are you just now telling me?" he demanded. Then, concerned, "No one was hurt, were they? You weren't hurt?"

"Of course not. And this is the first chance I've had to tell you," she added, a trace of impatience slipping into her voice. "You've been absorbed with the trial. And it really wasn't a big deal."

"Yeah, but trials come and go—"

"Now he tells me."

"No, really. You could've been hurt." He added, lowering his eyes, "I know I get pretty wound up sometimes, but—"

"You had no way of knowing. Really, it hardly caused a blip on the radar screen."

"You sure you're okay?"

"Perfect."

"So what happened?"

"A guy walked in with a note demanding money, the teller gave it to him, and he left. I was on the other side of the floor. I didn't even know it was happening until it was over."

He looked directly into her eyes. "Listen, baby. If anything like this ever happens again, I want to know about it—instantly. Okay? I don't care how absorbed I am. Deal?"

"Yes, sir." She raised her hand to her head in a salute, smiling broadly. He smiled back and gave her a long kiss. She was still savoring it when he attached his earphones and ran off. She stood, hands on hips, marveling at how he'd managed to get a head start, then attached her own earphones and sprinted after him to catch up. If they hurried, they could be home by eight and relax together in a hot shower.

Oblivious to the deepening darkness, Broadnax, traveling south on Lakeshore Drive, turned right onto East 55th Street. Barreling down the street with no headlights, he pressed the accelerator to fifty-five miles per hour in a thirty-five zone. He knew he was speeding, but the faster he went the more in control he felt. He was doing sixty-five now. He felt like he was riding on a cushion of air. Because traffic was light and the lanes wide, the car weaved from side to side, unchallenged for long stretches of roadway.

"Punch it, baby," he said, mimicking Steve McQueen in *The Getaway*. Ignoring the consequences, he floored the accelerator as Paul and JoAnne jogged onto East 55th from South Cornell Avenue a hundred yards ahead, their backs to traffic.

JoAnne saw the car first. She had playfully raced ahead of Paul and was looking over her shoulder to gauge the distance between them. When she saw it, she stopped in her tracks, ripped her earphones off, and reversed direction while frantically waving her arms above her head.

Broadnax had the vague sense that something was wrong and clumsily tried to regain control of the car. But his reflexes abandoned him. Like a drunken rodeo cowboy riding a bull he couldn't control, he hung onto the steering wheel with everything he had.

JoAnne screamed. Paul's mouth went dry. He'd seen that ghastly expression before, but never on his wife's face. The terror in her eyes was palpable. He yanked his earphones off as he whirled around and saw Broadnax's black SUV bearing down on him.

In a split second he calculated the awful aftermath. Instinctively he closed his eyes and his knees flexed in a futile attempt to get out of the way. But there was no time. No time to do anything but wait for the inevitable impact.

It wasn't what he expected. He felt a hard thud against his ribs, but it came from behind instead of in front, where the car should have crashed into him. JoAnne had reached him an instant before the car did, hurling her body into his across a space of ten feet and knocking him out of its path. His body absorbed the full force of hers, knocking the wind out of him. They hit the ground together, her on top, and as he rolled over on her she banged her head on the curb. Both lay dazed and stunned in the street.

In a few minutes Paul gathered his senses and pushed himself onto his hands and knees. He crawled the few yards that separated him from JoAnne and embraced her as she lay motionless. Then he sat up and pulled her close to his chest. After several agonizing seconds she stirred and opened her eyes. He grabbed her by both shoulders and gently eased her away from him so that his eyes could take in all of her.

"You okay?" he asked, heart racing.

"Yes, I think so. How about you?"

"Great, thanks to you."

She put her right hand on her forehead and grimaced.

"Are you sure you're okay?"

"My head hurts a little. I'll be fine."

"Do I need to tell you how much I love you?" he said sheepishly.

"Well, I finally found out what I have to do to get you to say it."

"Okay, okay, I love you," he said lightheartedly. Then he gazed into her eyes for a long moment. "Seriously, I do," he said, and meant it.

* * *

Broadnax lost control of his car a mile after he narrowly missed Paul and JoAnne, sideswiping cars on both sides of the street before flipping his over twice. Miraculously no one else was hurt and, as these things often happen, his injuries were relatively minor—a broken leg and a nasty gash on his forehead.

Paul felt good testifying against him. He felt even better when he was convicted and sentenced to a long prison term. But it wasn't enough. JoAnne never knew. Her funeral was two weeks earlier.

In the year since JoAnne's death, he had lived in a daze, attempting to confront his many demons. Once he'd regained his senses after the accident, he was stiff and sore but otherwise all right. By the time the ambulance arrived, JoAnne's headache had subsided. Paul tried in vain to convince her to go to the emergency room, to be safe, but she had an important meeting at work first thing in the morning and didn't want to run the risk that the hospital might keep her overnight for observation. Ironically, she was being as pig-headed about her job as Paul often was about his. He'd chuckled at that and even coaxed a smile out of her. In the end, they compromised. She promised that if her headache got worse she would drop everything and see a doctor immediately. But she never got a chance to make good on her promise.

He remembered vividly JoAnne's sudden restlessness during the night and the alarm he felt when she didn't respond to his frantic attempts to revive her. Without warning her head had started to throb, almost imperceptibly at first, and then ever more rapidly. As the throbbing quickened, so too did the pain until it finally felt like a miniature jackhammer boring a hole inside her skull. Before she could call out to Paul, there was an explosion inside her brain that he later learned had been caused by an aneurysm, and she lost consciousness.

That night she underwent surgery and for the next two months lay in a coma, attached to a respirator and clinging to life. The doctors offered little hope that she would ever regain consciousness and none that she could return to anything remotely resembling a normal life. Seventeen days before Broadnax's trial, JoAnne's parents and Paul jointly made the grim decision to disconnect the respirator. Within seconds she was gone.

JoAnne's surgeon had told him that even if she had been rushed to the hospital immediately after the accident, it was unlikely they could have saved her. Paul hadn't believed him. Although outwardly he had maintained his usual stoic façade, deep within he would not be consoled.

JoAnne died saving his life. Worse, she died because he'd insisted they go jogging to clear his head of a stupid trial. Sure, she had wanted to go in the end and they'd had a great time, but that wasn't the point. If it weren't for him, she wouldn't have been there.

And if she hadn't been there to save his life, would he have been killed, leaving her a widow? He knew how he should feel about that, but did he really? Yes, he did, he told himself over and over. That he could ever have doubted it, even for an instant, tormented him. He loved her deeply and would have gladly traded places with her.

Had JoAnne really known how much he loved her? It seemed clichéd, but he regretted now not having told her often enough. She'd joked about it on the night of the accident, and he realized too late how important a few words were.

From the point JoAnne was taken to the hospital Paul hid his distress. He had always viewed himself as being as solid as a rock—emotionally and physically. He didn't easily show his emotions and, inconsolable or not, he wouldn't now. He had learned from his father that men must be strong; that when they suffer they must do so silently, but then they must go on. So he kept his grief hidden and bound up tightly inside, struggling to break free but in no danger of doing so. At the funeral, although his eyes grew misty and the pain welled up inside him and fought to escape in a flood of tears, he didn't cry openly. Only when he returned to his apartment and faced the emptiness and silence did he allow himself to sob quietly in the darkness.

Paul went back to his job almost without a break, but it didn't work. He was distracted and struggled to concentrate. Once ensconced in his apartment he became a recluse, overdosing on old movies and rarely venturing out—with one exception.

Strangely, the one place he seemed to find solace was an indoor firing range that, despite JoAnne's mild protestations, he had frequented over the years to maintain his proficiency with the .45 automatic he'd learned to fire during his tour as an Army Reserve captain. Clutching the .45 in both hands, emptying the clip into the silhouette target, watching it slide slowly toward him, and seeing the holes clustered together in a tight pattern around the bull's-eye gave him a rush that, for a brief span, drowned out his grief. JoAnne hadn't understood this part of his psyche. He wasn't fascinated with the weapon, as she feared; he was intrigued by the challenge of mastering it, no less so than by the challenge of mastering the law. After much practice and dedication, he had succeeded.

For several months after the funeral Paul managed largely to keep his law partners at bay. But as the one-year anniversary of JoAnne's death approached, they staged an intervention of sorts, chipping in to fly him to an exotic locale for a needed break and dividing his cases among them so he'd have no excuse not to go. Reluctantly he agreed.

Paul had joined his law firm after he was married, and while he had fairly close relationships with many of the lawyers there, none were so close that anyone knew where he and JoAnne had spent their honeymoon. He decided not to spoil their surprise, and in late March he boarded the plane to sunny Honolulu.

* * *

Paul went directly from the airport to his hotel, where he settled into his room, which had a balcony overlooking the beach. Honolulu was breathtaking. He knew all about the tourist traps and tacky excesses, but the natural beauty of the place overwhelmed him once again. The beaches were dazzling, the sunrises spectacular, the sunsets glorious.

He spent the afternoon strolling the city streets, drinking in the sunshine and ambiance. The bustling streets in the city center weren't unlike those in Chicago, but in only a short distance they gave way to a tranquil oasis.

After his walk, Paul returned to the hotel and picked up *The Novels of Dashiell Hammett* he'd brought with him. He bought a straw mat from one of the numerous shops that sold them and headed for the beach, where he staked out a place in the shade for a few hours of reading. His concentration was broken only occasionally by the sight of all manner of women showing off firm bodies clad in colorful, skimpy bikinis.

For dinner he returned to a little restaurant and nightclub he'd seen earlier. A small sign on the wall outside announcing live music that night had caught his eye. The place was on the second level of a quaint little plaza tucked away in a quiet corner—the kind of place you could easily miss. It wasn't very busy and he pretty much had his pick of tables. He chose one near the back and off to the side. He ordered a Jack Daniels and water while he waited for his steak. They made their drinks strong and before long he felt warm inside.

As Paul nursed his drink, a female singer appeared on the small stage with a compact band of four—drums, guitar, saxophone, and keyboards. She was from the mainland and had shoulder-length, non-descript brown hair and an interesting, almost pretty face. She had a petite, firm figure covered by a knee-length, traditional Hawaiian flower-print dress that fit just tightly enough to leave something to the imagination.

She sang a few forgettable songs in a soft, lilting voice, revealing a talent that her material didn't completely disguise. Then she started singing "The Wind Beneath My Wings." Paul put his glass down and fixed his gaze on her. Something told him they would have made eye contact but for the dim light in the room. He liked the song well enough but it wasn't one of his favorites. In this setting and at this moment, though, something about it reminded him intensely of JoAnne.

They had met shortly after he graduated from college, at a time when his mind was still occupied by thoughts of someone who was always slightly beyond his grasp. A mutual friend introduced them at a party. They chatted a few minutes and went their separate ways. Neither seemed to have made an impression on the other.

After Paul graduated from law school, he flirted with the idea of moving out of his apartment and buying a house. Ironically, the same friend, who'd forgotten he'd introduced them years earlier, put him in contact with JoAnne to pre-approve his loan. When Paul saw her at the bank, seated at her desk, she looked familiar. "Do we know each other?"

"Paul Elliott, right?" She stood and extended her hand.

"Right," he said, taking it, embarrassed that he still couldn't place her and wishing the nameplate on her desk showed more than her last name. "And you're Ms.—"

"No need to be so formal, Paul." She smiled impishly.

"Okay, you got me."

"It's JoAnne."

"Right, right," he said as though he'd known all along. His eyes searched for her ring finger, but her arm rested behind her. He tilted his head to one side, but not discreetly enough.

"Is anything wrong?" she said, looking behind her.

"No." He shifted his own left arm behind his back. "Do you have the time?"

She consulted her watch on her left wrist and told him.

"Thanks. I don't want to be late for my next appointment." They both sat down. "I can't understand how I could have forgotten someone so attractive."

"Really?" she said slyly.

"Remind me where we were..."

"Don Kirkwood's party a few years ago. You do remember Don, don't you?"

"Of course. Don's the reason I'm here. But that explains it."

"Oh?"

"The lights were always too low at Don's parties. I was telling him that the other day."

"Come to think of it, I do remember being in the shadows, and what little light there was actually was directly over your head, which is why I got such a good look at you."

The banter flowed easily for several minutes before they got down to the business of mortgage options. When Paul got up to leave she said, "By the way, do you have the time?"

He looked at his left wrist and noticed his watch was partly visible at the edge of his jacket. He smiled broadly. "Got me again."

Paul stared beyond the singer at nothing in particular, smiling as he thought about the serene expression on JoAnne's face the night of the accident when he told her he loved her. In that instant he felt the weight of months of grief and struggle fall from his shoulders, and he was finally ready to let her go. She would have wanted it that way.

He waited for the song to end, paid for his uneaten meal, and left. Inside, he was still smiling.

* * *

Bright morning sunshine and a soft breeze flowing off the balcony through his hotel window conspired to awaken Paul from his morning slumber. He wiped the sleep from his eyes, stretched mightily, and took in copious breaths of sea-drenched air. He had been a decent athlete in college, running track, playing intramural lacrosse, and dabbling in Tae Kwan Do when he had time. He had stayed in shape, and now the slumbering muscles in his arms and legs also seemed to awaken.

He went to the window and looked out at the vast blueness of the still horizon that abutted the gently rolling ocean, dotted here and there with white-capped waves and tiny sailboats. *Life is good after all*, he thought.

After his breakthrough in the restaurant that first night, the next few days in Honolulu had been soothing but uneventful. He spent most of the time reading, relaxing on the beach, and sightseeing. He ate by himself in out-of-the way restaurants, content to be alone with his thoughts, but tonight he would make a change in his routine. A taxi driver had told him about the most authentic luau in town, and the bus stopped at his hotel. After the nights of solitude, he was ready for a change and he looked forward to the evening.

Chapter Eleven

After her talk with Robert—a scene Evelyn could only describe as bizarre—she decided to go to the gift shop to buy postcards. As she reached for a card that caught her eye, the revolving display spun quickly and she took a step back in surprise. Hearing her footstep and realizing what had happened, the man on the other side peered around the display to apologize, but Evelyn had already begun to look at other cards.

Paul was dumbfounded. With a broadening smile, he stared at her. Sensing his gaze, Evelyn looked in his direction and slowly let her eyes meet his. "Oh, my God! Paul, is that you?"

"Evelyn, how long has it been?"

"Oh, Paul!" She took a step toward him, opening her arms wide. He walked into her embrace and lingered. "How long?" she said when they separated. "Well, since you got married. That was—" He opened his mouth to speak, but she knew something was wrong. "Paul?"

"JoAnne died last year," he said with an equanimity that surprised him.

"I'm so sorry."

"No, no. I'm all better now. It took some time. Actually, coming here helped."

They stood there smiling, sizing each other up. "I still remember the last time we talked," Paul said.

Evelyn stared at the floor self-consciously. "To this day one of the most embarrassing moments of my life." They hadn't seen each other or even talked on the phone since college, and one day not long after he'd graduated from law school, she'd called out of the blue to ask him out. After hesitating a second while searching for a diplomatic response, he said straight out that he'd just gotten back from his honeymoon. "I don't even remember what I said after you delivered the news."

"You said 'Oh!' and hung up. What a twist of fate. I chased you off and on for three years in college, and the minute I get married you decide to give in. You must've been desperate."

"Paul! That is *so* not true. You were the first person on my list."

"Right. Tell me anything."

"I'm serious."

He took a step back and surveyed her from head to toe. She wore a colorful Hawaiian sundress with bursts of bright greens and yellows, and her long, dark hair was pulled back in a ponytail. "You haven't changed. You must be living right."

"Oh, I don't know about that," she said, as thoughts of Robert forced their way back into her consciousness. "But thanks for the compliment." He hadn't changed much either. Still fit and handsome in an understated way with the same probing eyes and ready smile. "You too."

"So...I suppose you married Robert."

"How'd you guess?" she said playfully.

Paul smiled. By the time he met Evelyn, he was already a pretty accomplished guy. But where she was concerned he'd never been able to compete with Robert. Paul was smarter, more authentic, and certainly more reliable, whereas Robert was impulsive, reckless, and, much as he hated to admit it, exciting—all of which had endeared him to Evelyn.

"I had a hunch," he said at last.

"Well, if you really want to know what happened, hearing about your marriage pushed me right into his arms," she joked.

"I'm sure," Paul said.

"It's a little more complicated," she said more seriously.

"And, of course, you're here with him."

"Well, sort of." Paul looked quizzical but waited. "Do you have a few minutes?"

"Sure."

"Can we go somewhere and talk?"

They walked to a cozy restaurant a few blocks off the main drag. Its interior was straight out of the late 1950s and early 1960s. A huge jukebox in the corner actually worked, and the walls were covered with photographs of entertainers from the dawn of rock and roll. They found a booth in the back and ordered Cokes.

Before telling Paul about Robert, Evelyn insisted on hearing about his marriage to JoAnne and what had brought him to Honolulu. When he had finished, she said how sad it was that JoAnne had died so tragically and that he'd blamed himself for so long, but also that she envied him for the wonderful times he and JoAnne had shared.

"I know it's bittersweet coming back here, but this is such a lovely place. You can't come here to mourn."

"Hear, hear." He lifted his glass, and hers touched it in a toast. "Now tell me about you."

She recounted her numerous problems with Robert, leading to her decision to come to Honolulu with Rachel and Robert's sudden decision to join them. "As you can see, I'm doing fine, all things considered."

"I hate to say I told you so," he joked, but she frowned. "So I won't. But I never understood what you saw in him."

She shrugged. "It was easier to see from your vantage point than it was from mine. He swept me off my feet, and when someone does that...well...you float about ten feet off the ground. And you don't see what's going on right in front of you. Or if you do, you know you can make it right if you try hard enough. Maybe you can sometimes, but most of the time you can't, no matter how hard you try."

Paul tried to understand how she felt, but it was a struggle because Robert's flaws seemed so much more obvious to him. Nevertheless, he hated that Robert had caused her so much misery, and he wished he could do something about it. He was about to tell her so when she surprised him.

"Anyway, it doesn't matter now. I think it's actually over this time."

"Really?" Paul said.

"Yes. It took me long enough to be able to say that. But yes, I'm serious." There was a momentary lull in their conversation, as each digested fully what the other had said. Then Evelyn broke the silence. "Paul," she said, leaning across the table toward him, "what are you doing tonight?"

He was more than a little unsure what she was getting at. "I'll have to check my calendar," he said, trying to elicit a smile from her. "Unattached man wandering around in paradise…who knows?"

She sat back and folded her arms in front of her chest. Her expression was like that of a teacher losing patience with the class clown.

"You found me out," Paul said. "I thought I'd take in a luau."

"What a coincidence! Rachel and I are going to a luau tonight and Robert thinks he's taking us to dinner, so I guess he's officially horned in. Why don't we all go together?"

"I don't know, Evelyn. Robert and I never—"

"Don't worry about him. Poor Rachel is in an awkward position, trying to referee us. She's only here because I pleaded with her to come. We shouldn't ruin her vacation. She's cute and sweet and, well, a little aggressive sometimes, but you'll like her." She paused, wondering whether she should add anything. "What do you think?"

Paul smiled impishly and crossed his own arms. "You aren't trying to fix me up?"

Evelyn had to smile. "An unattached man like you, wandering around paradise? Of course not. But you might have a good time, and maybe Rachel would, too."

"What about you?"

"Don't worry about me. I'll get through this thing with Robert. But thanks for asking. So what do you have to lose?"

"You think she might sweep me off my feet?"

"You never can tell."

"Okay, you win.

Chapter Twelve

Robert took the necklace to a small jewelry store he'd noticed a few blocks from the hotel. It was the best way he could think of to get an appraisal.

He had been looking over his shoulder ever since he got off the plane. When Evelyn noticed on the beach, he hoped his little joke had satisfied her. But he was jumpy and couldn't wait to find out whether his anxiety was justified, or whether he had been worrying himself to death over a piece of costume jewelry.

He should have been prepared. The stout, middle-aged jeweler with hooded eyes and dimpled cheeks looked immediately suspicious. He didn't say a word, but he didn't have to. The nervous clearing of his throat and the awkward loosening of his collar did the talking for him. Robert's explanation about a family heirloom intended as a gift for his wife was almost laughable. All he could do was pretend not to notice the jeweler's skepticism and curse himself for his carelessness. Of course, the necklace had to have been stolen. But having come this far, he had little choice but to see it through.

Even before lining up one of the stones under his loupe, the jeweler knew that the rubies were natural and had not been treated in any way. Under the loupe he could clearly see the fine inclusions, or bubbles, of rutile needles. Initially he was reluctant to estimate the value—first because he wasn't an appraiser and would have to guess, and second because he'd read about, but had never seen first-hand, color-matched pigeon-blood red rubies. But when Robert turned on the charm and gently pressed him for a ballpark figure, he relented. Merely providing that limited amount of information probably wouldn't render him an accomplice either to whatever Robert had already done or intended to do with the necklace.

When Robert heard the figure, which the jeweler insisted was only an estimate, it was all he could do to fake a polite smile and thank the merchant for his time. As he turned to leave, though, he felt his knees start to buckle, and it took a concentrated effort to steady himself. He thought he'd hidden his reaction well. He hadn't actually stumbled. And he complimented himself on having so seamlessly regained his composure.

Robert hurried back to the hotel, the encounter weighing heavily on his mind. He was comforted that the man hadn't insisted on any identification. If he did call the police they had no way of finding him.

It was time to call Litvak. Robert was plagued by doubt. *Is there any chance he hasn't figured out what happened? Is it possible I've been worrying myself sick for no reason?* There was one way to find out. He lay back on his bed and punched Litvak's number into his cell.

Litvak was at his desk reading a magazine when the phone rang. His secretary, who usually screened his calls, had stepped away.

"Frank, it's Robert."

"I've been expecting to hear from you. I'm glad you didn't disappoint me."

Shit! He knows. "What do you mean?"

"You know what I mean."

"I do?"

"Cut the bullshit. Where is it?"

Shit, shit! "Where is what?"

"I said cut the bullshit. You know goddamn well. Where is the necklace?"

"Oh, that. Why didn't you say so? I picked it up off the floor in the back of the car, and as we were driving along I was holding it, staring off into space and thinking about the mess I'd got into with you. On top of that, I was freaking out because I thought I'd be late for my flight. I had so much on my mind that when your guys dropped me off I completely forgot I had it in my hand. By the time I snapped out of it, they'd driven off."

Litvak was silent, so he kept talking.

"It turned out that I almost missed my flight. I only had time to finish packing and get to the airport. Believe me, I know nothing about jewelry, but I didn't figure the necklace was too valuable, considering where I found it. I thought maybe one of the guys had bought it as a gift for his girlfriend or something. I mean, how much could it be worth? I have a service come in and clean while I'm gone, so I didn't want to leave it in my apartment, because it might have some sentimental value and I didn't want it to come up missing. So I brought it with me. I thought I'd deliver it to you when I got back and you could return it to whoever owns it."

Here his saga ended, but this time he didn't have to wait for Litvak's reaction, which came swiftly.

"That's one hell of a story."

"It's the truth."

"Then why did you call? Obviously not about a necklace that might have some sentimental value to someone. Like you said, how much could it be worth?"

"I called to give you some news about the sale of the store."

"Let me guess. It couldn't wait till you got back."

"I thought you'd like to know."

"You are one slick motherfucker," Litvak said, almost with admiration. "No wonder I loaned you so much goddamn money."

"Don't you want to hear—?"

"You can tell me about it when you get back, which will be... "

"In about a week."

"And you are where?"

"In Miami, visiting friends." He didn't want to confirm that he was in Honolulu, and Miami was the first city that popped into his mind. "The weather's great down here."

"I'll bet."

"So, that necklace...sounds like it's worth more to somebody than I thought. I can FedEx it back if your guy can't wait. How much insurance? Five hundred dollars? A thousand?"

Litvak was so furious he could hardly contain himself, but he held his temper and responded in measured tones. "No, hang onto it. You were right. It's a keepsake. I wouldn't want to take a chance on it getting lost."

So Litvak knew how valuable it was. He hadn't doubted it much, but now he was sure. *So be it*, Robert thought. *They'll be coming for it.*

He wasn't overly concerned about Litvak sending men to Evelyn's school. He knew from experience that she didn't have to tell anyone where she was going, as long as they had her cell number. Rachel didn't have a lot of close friends there, and she was pretty discreet about her personal life. She was probably the one person who knew Evelyn was in Honolulu.

Sylvester Littlefield, his main store manager, was another matter. He had complained to him about Evelyn insisting on a trip to Honolulu and bragged about how he was going to get out of going. Littlefield even knew the date and time of her departure. Given his hasty explanation over the phone describing how he'd changed his mind at the last minute, he couldn't very well lie and say he was going to a different city. So Littlefield knew he was in Honolulu, but he didn't know where. He had to decide: Should he tell Littlefield or not?

He opted to split the baby. If he didn't tell Littlefield the name of the hotel, someone could put a gun to his head and make him call Robert on his cell (with who knew what consequences), and for the same reason he didn't instruct Littlefield not to tell anyone where he'd gone. He decided to give Littlefield the name of a hotel on the other side of town, the one where Evelyn had originally planned to stay before she peevishly upgraded after he refused to come along. If they were coming, that would at least slow them down—assuming they didn't call the hotel first. But why would they?

Litvak hadn't pressed him about being in Miami. Maybe they hadn't come by the store yet. He thought about calling Littlefield to find out whether anyone had come around looking for him, but he didn't want to know. If anyone had, it was too late to do anything about it. He had already checked for escape routes; there were no flights leaving the island until the next day.

What to do now? He didn't know exactly, but he had to share his good fortune with the woman he loved. Maybe together they could puzzle their way out of the dilemma he had created.

He punched a number into his cell. "Are you alone?"

"Yes," Rachel said. "She just left."

Chapter Thirteen

Sometimes it's better to be lucky than smart.

When Rico arrived in Honolulu and discovered Littlefield's information was wrong, he didn't have a clue where to start looking for Robert—but he asked the concierge where, besides his own fine establishment, a couple in their mid-thirties might make a reservation for a second honeymoon. It was a long list and Rico rewarded him with a hefty tip. He didn't relish having to go through the whole thing, but it was all he had. He located Robert's hotel on the seventh phone call. Lucky seven. And they had vacancies.

He didn't know whether Littlefield had been onto him, made an honest mistake, or was fed the wrong information by Robert. Right now it didn't matter.

After checking in, he went to his room on the sixteenth floor and laid his leather garment bag on the bed. He started to unpack but was immediately captivated by the panoramic ocean view and the waves rhythmically lapping the shore.

This was unexpected. The Pacific Ocean! No comparison to Chicago's Lake Michigan. Rico loved the grit and grime of Chicago, its sturdy skyscrapers, the hustle and bustle of life in the fast lane. But he wondered if he might get used to a place like this. Could Jean?

What the hell, he grumbled, snapping out of it. He called the hotel operator and had her ring Robert's room. No answer. He fixed a drink at the mini-bar and punched a number into his cell. "I'm here."

It sounded silly to say he was watching the ocean. "Yeah, I'm watching something—on TV. I'll be over in a few minutes." He opened the window to his balcony, walked outside, and stood sipping his drink and admiring the view.

* * *

Rico got out of the taxi in front of a small bungalow with a white picket fence in a quiet neighborhood a few miles from the town center. He opened the gate and went up the walk that divided the neatly mowed lawn. Before he could knock, the front door swung open and a large man appeared in the doorway—mid fifties, dressed in black pants and T-shirt, steel-gray hair pulled back in a medium-length ponytail. He motioned Rico inside with a tilt of his head.

As Rico crossed the threshold, the man headed past the sparsely furnished living room, down a short hallway, and into a bedroom barely large enough for its twin-sized bed, two modest side tables, and a rickety dresser. Rico closed the front door behind him and followed, stopping in the bedroom doorway. The man knelt, reached under the bed, and gently pulled a rug toward him. On it lay a brown leather briefcase whose fine craftsmanship contrasted sharply with the room's drab decor. He got to his feet, rested the briefcase on the bed, snapped open its twin locks, and raised the top to reveal its contents.

With a wave of his hand he invited Rico to take a seat on the bed next to the briefcase. He sat on the other side, angling the briefcase slightly in Rico's direction so he could get a better look inside. His first words were, "What do you think?"

"May I?" Rico asked. The man nodded. Rico removed a .45 Sig Sauer P226, a twelve-round-magazine-capacity, Swiss-designed semi-automatic assembled in Germany. A duplicate of the one he carried in Chicago. He knew a lot of guys who carried Glocks, but he preferred the Sig. At over two thousand dollars, it was an expensive weapon, known in some circles as the Rolls-Royce of pistols. That was reportedly why the Beretta 92F was selected over it in the 1980s when only those two pistols satisfactorily completed US Army trials. The Navy SEALs, however, later selected the P226 despite the cost. That was good enough for Rico.

Rico shifted the .45 quickly from one hand to the other to get a feel for it, held it out in front of him with both hands, stiff-armed, and sighted an imaginary target out the window. "Nice." He loaded a clip into the base and opened his lightweight sport coat, revealing the elastic blue shoulder holster he had brought with him from Chicago. He had had it a long time and it had sentimental value. If he couldn't have his own .45, at least he had this. He slid in the .45. Next, he removed a suppressor from the briefcase and held it up to the light from the window, examining it closely before returning it.

Finally, he reached in and, one piece at a time, pulled out a high-powered rifle. He assembled the parts and attached a scope. Once again, he sighted his target and held it for a long moment. Satisfied, he expertly disassembled the rifle and returned the pieces to their fitted compartments in the briefcase.

Rico stood and nodded to the man, who nodded back. Then he reached in his pocket and pulled out a wad of hundred-dollar bills. The man made a move to protest that it was too much. Rico raised a hand, palm out. "Keep it," he said. He closed the briefcase and snapped its locks. The man followed him to the front door and opened it, extending his hand. Rico shook it. "Later."

Chapter Fourteen

"So where's Evelyn?"

Rachel gripped the phone. She wanted to say that if he was so interested, maybe he should go out and look for her, but she restrained herself. For years Robert had chased other women, casually at first and lately with a vengeance, but Rachel had pursued him with the quiet, serious eye of a lioness. And now that she had him, she intended to keep him, but on her own terms.

She sighed, feigning exasperation. "Out making plans for us to go to a luau tonight."

"What?"

"She ran into some guy she knew in college, and the four of us are supposed to go. I didn't know what else to do, so I played along." Her frustration bubbled to the surface. "Which reminds me, it was more than a little awkward coming over here with her in the first place, and then to have you show up out of the blue…"

"Come on. Can't I catch a break? I explained all that."

"Yes, like you do everything."

"Can we change the subject?"

"If you insist."

He cringed. If he were a stronger man, he would have broken it off with her long ago when he realized that she wouldn't allow herself to be shunted aside like the others. Beneath the deceptive façade she showed Evelyn and the rest of the world, she was as tough as nails and every bit as manipulative as he was. But it was too late now. He didn't know what she was selling, but whatever it was, he had bought it and he needed it like a junkie needs his next fix.

"Sit down and listen," he said. "I've got something important to tell you."

He described his encounter with the jeweler, omitting the man's suspicion. When he said what the necklace might be worth, she gasped. "But now I have to deal with Litvak."

"Fuck Litvak," she said calmly.

The words were spoken with such nonchalance that they took Robert by surprise. "What?"

"You heard me. I said fuck him."

"Hold on. This isn't a guy you can cross without thinking twice."

"Oh, but you already did, my dear."

"Don't be so goddamn flip. This is the real deal. It's got to be handled right."

"Listen, it's simple. Either you give it back or you keep it. There's no in between."

It was becoming a test of wills. "You don't know that."

"Trust me, I do."

"I'm going to give him a call."

"You're not serious!"

"It's worth a shot."

Exasperated, Rachel closed her eyes. "Okay. But at least wait till I get there."

"You remember that little park down the street from the hotel?"

"Yes, I know it."

"Be there in twenty minutes." But before he disconnected, he had to ask, "What's the name of the guy from college?"

"I don't remember. Why?" She did remember and had an idea why Robert asked.

"Curiosity."

"Paul something or other."

"Elliott?"

"You remember him then?"

"Oh, yeah," he said with relish, smiling to himself.

"What is *that* supposed to mean?"

"It means I'll see you in twenty minutes."

* * *

Despite his reticence when Evelyn invited him to the luau, Paul now looked forward to going. It was true that she had repeatedly rejected his advances in college, only agreeing to go out with him when she and Robert hit an inevitable rough patch. They'd had good times, full of innocent, youthful exuberance. Paul still had a picture of them in his dorm room posing together, his arm around her waist, each with a drink in their free hands, toasting some forgotten event and smiling radiantly. But those times had been as brief as they had been rare.

So he had moved on to other relationships. Some had been fun, even exciting, but until JoAnne, none were meaningful or fulfilling and none had lasted. Part of the reason was Evelyn. Still, for long stretches of time when he didn't see her, she rarely entered his mind. But when she did, he couldn't get her out, even after college and well into law school, and he wondered endlessly what she saw in Robert that she couldn't see in him. Obviously, she wasn't drawn to the earnest young man Paul was then. And Paul had to admit that to a remarkable degree, he remained the same person today.

He showered and put on a Hawaiian shirt. He allowed himself to preen in the mirror a little. It would be an interesting evening.

* * *

The park where Robert and Rachel agreed to meet was tiny, fewer than four- or five-hundred-yard square, but it was a leafy oasis in the middle of a bustling downtown. He was waiting on a bench when she arrived. She was barely three minutes late but he glanced at his watch to show his disapproval.

"I got here as fast as I could," she said, irritated, and sat beside him.

"Don't worry about it." He took out his cell phone.

"What are you going to tell him?"

"Just listen." He punched in Litvak's number and she listened in. "It's me again, Robert."

"I know who it is," Litvak barked.

"Listen, I bumped into a jeweler in the hotel lobby right after we talked, by coincidence, you know, and one thing led to another and he asked if he could take a look at the necklace. I said why not and, long story short, well, I couldn't believe my ears." He winked at Rachel.

"Spit it out."

"From the way you acted, I wasn't sure you knew."

"Well, now you are."

"Okay, then for something worth that much, don't you think I deserve...well, a finder's fee or something?"

"You little prick. You trying to shake me down?"

"Of course not! But from the way the jeweler looked at it, I'm sure he thought I stole it. I mean, I would never mention your name, but he knows I'm staying at the hotel and if he calls the police..."

"You're not that stupid."

Now Robert stammered. "All I'm saying is...if I hadn't found it, it could've fallen out of the car...or who knows what. I think that's worth something."

"No fucking way. The way I see it, it didn't get up and walk into your pocket. You don't deserve shit."

"What I'm saying is—"

"Not a goddamn penny."

With every insult Rachel grew progressively angrier. Clearly Robert had lost control of the conversation. To his astonishment, she grabbed the phone and screamed into it, "Hey! You wanna be like that? Well, fuck you! We'll take it all, you son of a bitch. And if you try anything, we'll turn it over to the cops!"

Flabbergasted, Robert froze.

"Who the hell's this?" Litvak shouted.

"Don't worry who this is! When you wanna talk, you know how to reach us." She disconnected.

Robert jumped to his feet, ripped the phone from her hand, and stared at her in disbelief. "Woman, what the fuck are you doing?"

She stood her ground. "Didn't you hear him? He blew you off."

"Goddamn it, I don't care what he said. I told you, you don't cross him."

"And I told you there's no middle ground."

Something clicked in Robert's brain. "You planned that, didn't you?" he said calmly.

She was as cool as he was. "I knew what he was going to say. I told you that."

"All right, Miss Know-It-All. Now what?"

"We leave. Start fresh someplace."

"You don't know him. He'll find us."

"Not if we're smart."

"You have all the answers."

"I try," she said smugly.

"You ready never to see Chicago again?"

"No big loss. There're plenty of Chicagos."

"I had a lot tied up in those stores."

"They were both taking on water faster than you could bail it out."

"It was more than money, you know that," he said. But slowly, inexorably, he began to catch up to her. "I have to think." He paced, back and forth.

"There's nothing to think about. Either we do this or we don't. Unless…"

"Unless what?"

"There's one thing left for you in Chicago besides those stores."

"I told you. That's over. You know that."

"Is it?"

He took her in his arms and kissed her passionately. "Does that answer your question?"

Chapter Fifteen

Rico returned to his hotel room to relax and wait for Litvak to call. Once again, he was drawn to the balcony, transfixed by the vast ocean below. He wouldn't have been able to explain it. He was simply mesmerized by the tranquility of it all. *I guess that's why they call it the Pacific.*

He left his .45 in the room safe and went down to the beach. He took off his shoes and socks and rolled up his pant legs. And when his bare feet started to burn, he trotted, then loped toward the lapping waves until his feet met the cool, wet sand. Again, thoughts of Jean intruded. *I must be getting old.*

His cell rang. "Speak."

"Bobby found out what he's holding," Litvak said. "The lying son of a bitch called and said he's in Miami. It looks like he grew some balls, too—or at least his wife did."

"What do you mean?"

" 'Fuck you,' she said. Well, fuck her!"

"Don't worry. He won't have it for long. But after this don't call me. When I get it I'll let you know."

Before Rico could disconnect, Litvak said, "Hold on. I want to send a message."

"Meaning?"

"They don't walk away from this."

"The woman too?"

"*Especially* the woman."

"You sure about that?"

"Stop asking questions. Just do it."

Rico went to a nearby bar and had a drink. From his seat he could still see the massive blue ocean outside and the surf crashing against the shore. He wished Jean were there. He pictured her smiling beside him, fiery red hair catching the wind. He chuckled. "I gotta get away from this goddamned ocean."

Then business intruded. He paid for his drink, went outside, turned his back to the beach, and headed for the city streets.

Rico was a killer with a conscience. He had two kinds of boundaries: those he wouldn't cross under any circumstances and those he would rather not cross if he could avoid it. The distinction was impossibly imprecise, and only he could define it. It didn't matter what anybody else thought. A thing had to feel right to him. Killing a child, for instance, didn't feel right. So he would never do it. Ever.

Killing a woman, on the other hand, was a different matter. He would prefer not to kill this woman, but he would do it if it couldn't be avoided. Unfortunately for her, it didn't look like it could be.

* * *

Robert had dressed for the luau and was taking a final look at himself in the bathroom mirror when the phone rang. He went to the bedroom and answered it.

"Room 433?" Rico asked in a cultured voice. No hotel switchboard anywhere in the world will give anyone the room number of a hotel guest, even if the person inquiring is another guest. He counted on Robert correcting him.

Instead Robert said, "No, you have the wrong number."

"My apologies," Rico said, "but there must be a problem with the switchboard. This is the third time they've connected me to the wrong room. Would you mind telling me your number so I can report it to the operator?"

Robert didn't suspect a thing. "No problem. This is 913."

"Thanks very much." He slid the Sig into his shoulder holster, slipped it on, covered it with his jacket, and headed for room 913.

Chapter Sixteen

Paul arranged to meet Evelyn and Rachel in the hotel lobby. It was a lofty space bedecked with crystal chandeliers, marble floors, and modern artwork that screamed money and whispered elegance. He arrived a few minutes early, so he took a seat in one of the plush armchairs and watched the cavalcade of people from all over the globe pass before him, all with an air of self-assurance that erased any doubt they belonged exactly where they were. A partner in his law firm for over three of his ten years there, he had grown comfortable in that milieu, and in this one. His success and hard work allowed him to vacation in places like this and not feel the least bit uncomfortable or out of place. It hadn't always been so.

His mother's parents had migrated from the South in search of a better life, steady employment, and most of all, freedom from Jim Crow. They both worked in the cotton fields of Arkansas during various parts of the school year for much of their childhoods and neither had the chance to finish high school, much less college, but they were determined that Paul's mother and her three siblings would.

And they did. His mother became a registered nurse, a sister and a brother became teachers, and another sister became a social worker.

Paul's father was an auto mechanic. His grandparents had hoped their daughter would marry someone with a professional background and were wary of his father at first, but he was a conscientious and loving husband, and they grew to like and respect him. Paul's parents were neither poor nor well off, and everyone chipped in to help with the family finances. Paul had three brothers and two sisters, and he and his brothers all had paper routes or other part-time jobs at one time or another, while his sisters regularly found work babysitting.

Although a good student in high school, he hadn't been challenged academically. It took him nearly two years of hard slogging to adjust in the very selective Midwestern college he attended, where even the laggards seemed at least as bright as he was. He grew up in a lower middle class segregated neighborhood that, while not as rough as some, still had its share of challenges. Soon enough, more out of necessity than desire, he learned how to handle himself like everyone else. But he was never an instigator—except once. From the instant it happened, he regretted it.

He was more of a student than anyone else in the neighborhood group that made up his circle of friends away from school. That occasionally put pressure on him to prove that he was "one of the guys." One way was to start a fight with some hapless person when egged on by the group.

One day when Paul was thirteen or fourteen, a group of boys goaded him into provoking a fight with a boy who lived on the corner of Paul's street. The boy was a little effeminate and the neighborhood boys often teased him and called him "sissy." Paul was reluctant to act the part of a bully but not enough to ignore his friends. Before he knew it, he was confronting the boy amidst a sea of onlookers urging him on. Not waiting for Paul to take the first swing, the boy advanced toward Paul, closed his eyes, and started swinging both arms wildly like an out-of-control windmill.

Paul pivoted to one side, grabbed the boy in a bear hug, and wrestled him to the ground. Then he took hold of the boy's wrists and held them down.

Reliving the incident as he waited in the hotel lobby, Paul looked into the face of the boy lying pinned to the ground, but the person he saw was Robert grinning back at him triumphantly.

"Paul." Evelyn tapped him on the shoulder. "You looked far away."

"I was." He stood and got his first look at Rachel. She was attractive, not as petite as Evelyn, with short, curly hair and a saucy smile. Her form-fitting pants would have got his attention more than they did if he weren't so taken with Evelyn. "Hi, I'm Paul." He took her hand.

"Nice to meet you," Rachel said.

"My pleasure. Is Evelyn keeping you out of trouble?"

"Like my mother."

"I'll let that one slide," Evelyn said.

"Where's Robert?"

"Oh, I forgot to tell you, Evelyn," Rachel said. "He called while you were in the bathroom. He's running a little late. He'll meet us on the bus."

"Same old Robert," Paul quipped.

* * *

Rico got on the elevator and watched the illuminated numbers above the doors mark its descent to the fourteenth floor. The doors opened, two people got on, and the elevator resumed its journey to the ninth floor, where Rico got off and walked to room 913. After checking to his left and right, he stood to one side so he couldn't be seen through the peephole, and knocked. No answer. He knocked again. Then he hurried to the elevator. An empty car arrived quickly. He pushed the button for the lobby. As the elevator descended past the third floor, seconds from the lobby, another elevator arrived there. The doors parted and Robert and three other passengers stepped out. Robert could see the tour bus parked outside. He started in that direction at the same moment the doors to Rico's elevator opened, giving Rico an unobstructed view of his target.

But it was already too late. Making an attempt here would be foolhardy. And Rico wasn't sure where the necklace was. Added to that, he had the woman to worry about. Getting a second crack at her would be difficult after taking her husband out here, even if it made sense, which it didn't. He had no choice. The thing would have to wait.

As Robert neared the bus, Rico got the attention of a desk clerk walking by and asked where the bus was headed and whether he could get there by cab. Assured that he could, he meandered over to the sliding glass doors, folded his arms across his chest, and watched the bus pull away.

Chapter Seventeen

Paul watched Robert climb onto the bus. After ten years at the law firm he was practiced at dealing with awkward situations, and worse. Once, as an insecure young associate anxious to make a good impression, he took a call from a client he'd never met face to face but had talked to by phone a few times. After Paul solved his legal problem, the client asked out of the blue what Paul could do to help him keep "the blacks" from moving into his neighborhood. Awkward indeed.

Paul's response was a cold silence as the wheels in his brain, in search of the right words, spun like a roulette wheel. But before the words could take shape in his mind, his silence had evoked more consternation in the client's psyche than mere words ever could have.

In a quiet panic, the client had stammered, "You—you aren't black, are you?"

"Yes, I believe I am."

He started to apologize profusely and, as the seconds ticked by, more and more clumsily. When the silence was too much he hung up. The partner responsible for the client brushed the episode aside and told Paul to forget about it. The times had changed but some people never would. The law firm had changed, too, embracing Paul as one of its own, but the client remained a client.

Another time, when he wasn't yet a partner, on punishingly short notice he had to take over a medical malpractice case from the firm's star trial lawyer. The man had burned himself out trying a string of high-pressure cases back to back all over the country and couldn't take another without a break. The client, a surgeon, as solipsistic as he was brilliant, wasn't happy, and who would be? Paul handled it by suppressing his inner turmoil, presenting a calm façade, and methodically winning the case. Only his closest associates ever knew what a stomach-churning experience it had actually been. Viewed through the prism of time, the case itself, he later recognized, hadn't been nearly as challenging as it seemed then.

Compared to these and a dozen more experiences, putting up with Robert for an evening didn't merit a second thought. He forced a smile as Robert made his way toward him. He'd have to make a greater effort to contain his dislike for the man than he'd anticipated. It was good to see Evelyn again, and if this was the price of admission, he would pay.

Paul was in an aisle seat next to Rachel, who was directly behind Evelyn, reading a book. As Robert approached, he stood to shake hands. "It's been a while."

Robert grabbed his outstretched hand and pulled him in for a man hug, greeting him like a long-lost buddy. "Great to see you, man." Robert smiled broadly and patted Paul's back.

"Good to see you, too," Paul said, trying to muster some sincerity. He was taken aback by the effusive show of affection, although, knowing Robert as he did, he shouldn't have been. Vying for the affections of the same woman, they'd been anything but close in college. Same old Robert, the consummate salesman, perennially upbeat even without a reason.

"How are you and Rachel getting along?"

"Fine."

"Is that right, Rachel?"

"Of course. Don't you believe him?" She was a tad too sarcastic, causing Paul to raise an eyebrow, but Robert hardly noticed.

"Listen, Paul, we'll catch up when we get there." He eased into the seat next to Evelyn and whispered, "Look at this guy. Same old Paul. Hasn't changed a bit." She looked up for a second, smiled pleasantly, and went back to reading.

* * *

Rico undressed down to his briefs and slipped on the complimentary bathrobe. He put the room card key and his wallet in the pocket, along with his .45, and picked up the ice bucket. Then he took the elevator to the ninth floor and called the front desk on the house phone.

"Hello, this is Robert McDuffie in 913. I feel really stupid, but I've locked myself out of my room. I'm in the hall wearing a robe. Could you send somebody up to let me in?"

"Certainly, Mr. McDuffie. Someone will be right up."

He filled the ice bucket while he waited. The bellman arrived in three minutes.

"I feel like such a klutz," Rico said. "I went down the hall for ice and forgot my key card."

"That's all right. It happens a lot." And it did, so he wasn't at all suspicious. Besides, a man careless enough to leave his key card in his room couldn't be expected to be carrying identification to pick up ice.

Even so, Rico had planned to reassure him. Once the door was open he stepped to the side, so that it hid the right side of his body and most of the nearby bureau, and adroitly removed his wallet and key card from his robe. "Wait a second while I get my wallet." He put them on the bureau an instant before he opened the door enough for the bellman to see him pick them up.

"That's really not necessary," the bellman protested lightly.

"Oh, I insist. This is for you. Thanks again." He handed him a twenty and he left.

Rico searched the room thoroughly. Nothing. Even the room safe was open and empty. *Maybe it's in the hotel safe, or she's wearing it.* He guessed the latter, from the way Litvak described her, but it had made sense to check while they were gone.

He called the front desk. "This is Mr. McDuffie in 913. While I was taking a nap, my wife stepped out and I can't reach her on her cell phone. I bought her a necklace today for our anniversary and we talked about keeping it in the hotel safe, but something tells me she forgot to sign it in. I'd feel a lot better if I knew. Could you check for me, please?"

"Hold one moment, please.

"I'm sorry, sir, but the necklace isn't registered. Can I do anything else?"

"No, thanks. I'm probably overreacting. I'll catch up with her soon." As he reached the door to go he realized he hadn't seen a single item of women's clothing or toiletries. Why would Robert and Evelyn be staying in separate rooms? He made up his mind to go at the last minute. *Sounds like she's pissed.* Well, he didn't have time to find her room or dream up another ruse to get in. Right now it made sense to go straight to the source. He went back to his room and changed into something suitable for a luau.

Chapter Eighteen

After a twenty-minute drive, the bus arrived at a picturesque forest clearing lit by dozens of tiki torches, the ocean and setting sun as a backdrop. Male and female Hawaiian dancers, bare-chested men and women in coconut-shell bras, greeted everyone with colorful traditional leis and led them on a pre-dinner trek. Throughout the area and along shallow dirt trails fanning out like the spokes of a wheel were photos and artifacts depicting slices of life in the island's long history.

During dinner under a moonlit sky, guests from several tour buses, seated at white-linen-covered tables, were treated to an elaborate floor show. It began with a chorus of enchanting hula dancers with undulating bellies and gyrating hips that enthralled the men in the audience and impressed the women, and culminated in an intricate routine performed by a man whose sole prop was a baton that sprouted flames at both ends. He twirled it nimbly between the fingers of both hands before tossing it impossibly high in the air again and again and catching it each time behind his back with one hand.

When the show was over, a band played and couples made their way to the hardwood dance floor, inlaid perfectly against the forest bed in front of the stage.

Conversation between the foursome during dinner was limited as everyone concentrated on the stage show. Liquor had flowed freely, though mostly in Robert's direction. Paul noticed that Robert's drinking displeased both Evelyn and Rachel. Clearly neither liked it, and judging from their expressions, Rachel liked it even less than Evelyn did.

Since Robert had made a big deal out of Evelyn wearing the necklace to the luau, he had Rachel deliver it to her to keep up appearances. She had disagreed but humored him so it would never be out of her sight.

Evelyn indeed wore it, though not for Robert's benefit. She happened to have a form-fitting, fiery red Hawaiian dress she had been saving for a special occasion and the necklace complemented it perfectly. Paul and Robert both were bowled over by it and said so, which didn't please Rachel. Not particularly looking forward to the luau and not needing to impress anyone, she wore a simple pair of slacks (albeit so tight that it looked like she had been poured into them) and an unspectacular matching blouse with a high collar.

Paul had noticed the necklace immediately when he got on the bus but had waited until now to say anything. "That's a lovely necklace. It really goes well with your dress."

"Thank you," she said smiling, and with less enthusiasm, "It's a present from Robert."

"It *is* a good match," Rachel said.

"Would you like to try it on?" Evelyn said.

"May I?"

"Of course." Evelyn took it off and handed it to her.

"I always knew you had excellent taste in women," Paul said to Robert. "It looks like that applies to jewelry, too."

"I always knew you had excellent taste in women, too," Robert replied, taking a healthy swig from his drink. "And I don't just mean Rachel, your lovely blind date."

"Oh, I don't know about that..."

"What? Isn't Evelyn still your type?"

"Robert!" Evelyn gasped. "You've had too much to drink."

"You know anything about jewelry, Paul?" he continued.

"A little."

"Only a little? Back in college you knew so much about everything."

It made little sense to get into a pointless argument with Robert, who by then had consumed a prodigious amount of liquor. "Coming from you, Robert, that's a compliment," he said smiling.

"Well, let me tell you something about that necklace I bet you *don't* know," he said, pointing a finger at the necklace around Rachel's neck.

"Robert!" Rachel shouted, startling Evelyn and Paul. "Cool it, okay?"

"Thank you, Rachel," Evelyn said, though puzzled by the intensity of her friend's reaction.

"Thank you, Rachel," Robert mimicked.

"Robert—" Evelyn began.

"Okay. I'll be good." He finished his drink and gestured for another.

* * *

Minutes earlier Rico had arrived and spotted the couples from several yards away. He circled until he faced Rachel, removed a photo from his shirt pocket, and studied it briefly—the same picture that had fallen out of the duffel bag at Robert's apartment when he and Jerry searched the place. His eyes shifted between the necklace around Rachel's neck and the photo, which showed her and Robert dressed for a night out, beaming and holding hands like lovers. He put the picture back in his pocket and disappeared into the night.

* * *

"So, Evelyn, I don't think you ever mentioned Paul." Rachel made her voice calm.

"It was quite a surprise running into him here." Evelyn was still unsettled by Rachel's earlier display. "We haven't seen him since he graduated and left Robert and me behind."

"There *was* a phone call, though," Robert sneered. "We mustn't forget the phone call."

"Are you okay, Robert?" Paul asked. "Because if not, this is going to be a long evening."

Robert's eyes narrowed and his jaw tightened.

"Leave him to me, Paul," Evelyn said quietly and turned to Rachel. "Do you want to take Paul for a spin around the dance floor?"

What Rachel wanted was to have it out then and there, but she was so angry she feared she might say or do something else in the heat of the moment that she'd later regret. Robert had made and broken the same promises to her that he'd made to Evelyn about controlling his drinking. To make matters worse, at the same time he was supposed to be starting a new life with her, here he was competing with Paul over Evelyn like a jealous schoolboy. She had had fair warning, but now she wondered what she was getting into, and she resolved at that moment that whether or not she stayed with Robert, she would somehow get her hands on the necklace.

She stood and offered her hand. "Paul?"

"Of course." He led her to the dance floor.

When they were out of earshot, Evelyn said, "Where did *that* come from?"

"You tell me," Robert said petulantly.

"After all you've put me through, you have the nerve to be jealous over a phone call that took place more than ten years ago when you and I weren't even together?"

"A phone call you happened to tell me about for the first time today. I'm not jealous. I'm pissed. How do I know it was *one* phone call?"

"And what if it wasn't? After all your women, how can you talk?"

He tried to hide his astonishment by staring past her, refusing to look in her eyes.

"Is *that* what's bothering you?" she asked. "You think your sweet little Evelyn may have actually had an affair, and despite your own serial infidelities, you can't bear the thought of it? That's it, isn't it?"

She stood. "You know what? I was waiting for a more appropriate time, but after your performance tonight, you can have your next conversation with my lawyer." She started to walk away.

"That'd be Paul, I suppose, or doesn't he handle divorces?" She turned and glared at him and he grinned, drunk and malevolent. "By the way, in case you're wondering, your good friend Rachel is the other woman. One of them, anyway." It shook her to the core. *Not Rachel! How could I have been so blind? And so stupid?* She bit her lip, trying to maintain her composure. She had planned to sit at another table to wait for Paul, but now she hurried to the dance floor. Rachel was facing the other way, but Paul saw a determined look he'd never seen before as she marched up and tapped Rachel on the shoulder.

"I'm cutting in," she said angrily.

"What?" Rachel managed to say.

"How *could* you?!"

Rachel looked for Robert through the dancing couples blocking her view. Then she saw his ugly smirk and she knew. Their eyes met and he shrugged and lifted his glass. *Well, it's out of my hands now. All the cards are on the table. No reason to hold back.*

"Grow up, Evelyn. You're better off without him. If it hadn't been me, it would've been somebody else." As she pushed past, Evelyn clasped her arm. "What *now?*"

"I'll take my necklace." She held out her hand.

"You will, will you?"

"It *is* mine." Evelyn surprised herself by holding her ground.

Rachel knew Evelyn too well to suspect that she would physically try to wrest it from her. But she also knew she was trying to save face. After tonight's revelations the last thing she'd want was a reminder of Robert, no matter how expensive. She was too proud, too independent, and too oblivious to money. She would probably return it after she cooled off, maybe as soon as she got back to the table. The next morning at the latest. The only reason to keep it was spite. She'd shown some spunk tonight, but spiteful she was not.

Even if she was wrong about Evelyn, she knew how to get the necklace back when they were alone. Evelyn might be too refined to get physical, but Rachel certainly wasn't. Rachel smiled confidently.

"Yes, it's yours." She unclasped it and handed it to her. "If you want a daily reminder of a snake like Robert hanging around your neck, be my guest." She left to rejoin him.

"You know, she's right," Evelyn said. "I have no intention of keeping it—or anything else of his." She lowered her eyes to look at it and contemplate what had happened.

Paul had watched the scene with a mixture of surprise and bemusement. He didn't quite know why, but he was proud of her. He lifted her chin with the back of his index finger and looked in her eyes. "Put that thing on and let's dance."

* * *

As Rachel rejoined Robert, Rico reached the secluded spot above the clearing, seventy-five yards away, where he'd hidden the rifle in the undergrowth. From his perch he saw their animated discussion. He donned leather gloves, opened the case, and assembled the rifle.

* * *

"If you can't hold your liquor, don't drink," Rachel said. Robert lifted his glass for a gulp and she grabbed his wrist. He didn't resist as she guided it to the table. "What am I missing? What the hell do you care how she feels about him? You want to blow this?"

"Why did you give it back?" Robert said, as though he were inquiring about the weather.

"Because I didn't want to make a bigger scene than you already had. She was being a bitch. In a few minutes she'll march over here and throw the damn thing in your face—or mine." She looked at him contemptuously. "Jesus Christ! Maybe I'm the one who's making a mistake."

Chapter Nineteen

Cradling the rifle in his arms, Rico lay prone on the forest floor and adjusted the scope until his target was in the crosshairs. Robert's right temple looked close enough to touch.

* * *

Robert wasn't drunk enough to be invulnerable to the scorn in Rachel's voice. "That was my last drink," he said, chastened. But she'd heard that song before. Under raised eyebrows she cast him a dubious glance. "No, I mean it this time. That's it. Absolutely my last—"

Robert's head snapped to one side and his body, as though launched by a slingshot, flew out of his chair and hit the ground. All music and motion abruptly halted as scores of eyes searched the night, trying to understand the crackle that had pierced the air. Then someone yelled, "A gunshot!" and there was pandemonium. People scattered in all directions, some shrieking and screaming, others too terrified to speak.

Rico's scope followed Rachel as she leaped to her feet. Her eyes were frozen on Robert's body, lying motionless at her feet, blood oozing from an ugly bullet hole in his temple. She gasped once, twice, three times, but no sound escaped her. Then the same awful sound rang out again and her head flew backward, leading the rest of her body to the ground.

Rico rose quickly and donned his sunglasses. After years of wearing them at night, his eyes adjusted quickly. He reached under his jacket, un-holstered his .45, and unscrewed the silencer so that the next shots he fired would create maximum panic. Leaving the rifle and case, he jogged toward the bodies, pushing his way past the panicked people who blocked his path.

Paul had pulled Evelyn to the floor and covered her body with his own. "Where did it come from?" she whispered. Then three more gunshots rang out.

Four brave souls, three men and a woman, had gone to the victims to try to help. When they heard the shots, two of the men ran while the woman and the other man fell to the ground.

"Move!" Rico shouted as he reached them, and the two Samaritans scrambled to their feet and, without looking back, ran like frightened wildebeests with a pride of hungry lions in hot pursuit.

Paul carefully rose to a kneeling position and slowly looked around, three hundred sixty degrees. He and Evelyn were the only ones remaining on the dance floor, but he could see several people in the distance. Cautiously he stood and helped Evelyn to her feet. They looked toward their table.

Rico, out of their line of sight, knelt over Rachel and lowered her high collar. *What the hell?* He'd been facing her when he saw her wearing it, but when he took the shot her back was to him and he couldn't see it. *Did it come off?* He quickly scoured the area on hands and knees. He reached for her purse lying on the table and rifled through it. No luck.

He frisked Robert's body. Same result.

Now what? He didn't know but he knew he had to get out of there. By now fifty cell phones had called 911.

As he got to his feet, his back was facing Paul and Evelyn, not twenty-five yards away. "That's our table," Evelyn said and, without stopping to think, she bolted toward Rico.

"Evelyn!" Paul shouted and started after her.

In that instant, a tiny middle-aged woman, hiding in the shadows after being separated from her husband, appeared out of nowhere and crashed into Paul. She fell to the stage floor. With one eye on Evelyn, he helped her to her feet and ran after Evelyn.

Hearing Paul's voice, Rico, the .45 at his side, turned to face Evelyn. Seeing the gun, she stopped in her tracks and the color drained from her face. She caught a glimpse of his face, draped in sunglasses, but mostly she saw the .45. Since she was blocking Paul's view as he came up quickly behind her, he didn't see what happened next. She saw it as a blur.

Rico thrust both arms out and up in front of him, his left hand joining his right around the butt of the gun. As his arms came level with his shoulders, they snapped to a stop, the abruptness of which caused Evelyn to flinch. As she came into focus, staring anxiously into the barrel of the Sig Sauer, the slightest smile creased his face and the muscles in his arms relaxed. As swiftly as he'd hoisted it, he holstered the .45, turned on his heel, and disappeared once more into the darkness that had obscured the necklace around Evelyn's neck.

Paul reached Evelyn the second Rico turned away. He took her hands in his. She was shivering and her heart was racing. He embraced her and she held on tightly. She took some deep breaths until her pulse started to return to normal. Then she took a step back and wiped a tear from her eyes.

"Better?" Paul asked gently. She nodded. "That had to be the one doing the shooting. Did you get a look at him?"

"No. I mean, barely. He was wearing sunglasses. It's dark. But I saw the gun."

"Damn," Paul said under his breath.

People started trickling back from various hiding places and Paul and Evelyn saw them gather around their table.

"Oh, my God!" Evelyn shouted.

Paul got there first and, pleading with Evelyn, tried in vain to keep her from getting close enough to see the carnage. When she did, she dropped to her knees, buried her face in her hands, and wept. Paul knelt beside her, took her in his arms once more, and let her cry.

Carrying the rifle case, Rico left the thicket for an empty taxi parked off the road in a small clearing concealed by heavy vegetation. He opened the trunk, revealing a frightened taxi driver, bound and gagged and drenched in sweat. "So far, so good." He tossed in the case, got behind the wheel, eased the car out of its hiding place, and drove off.

Minutes later, as he cruised down the highway, a police car sped toward him in the opposite lane, followed in rapid succession by another, lights flashing and sirens screaming. Rico held his breath until they whizzed by.

He parked on a quiet, dimly lit street on the outskirts of the city. He retrieved the case from the trunk, then propped it open with a folded newspaper and told his passenger, "Don't move until you see daylight."

He walked three blocks and hailed another taxi, which took him back to his hotel. Once in his room he lay across the bed and pondered what had happened.

Chapter Twenty

Rico had counted on the guests turning away in horror and panic as the murders unfolded before them. If any managed not to avert their gaze, he expected them to watch from a safe distance, too far away to get a good look at him—even if the lighting were better and even if his face weren't partially shielded by sunglasses.

He was right. Of the dozens of people the police interviewed that night, only a handful caught even a glimpse of the gunman's face, and their descriptions varied so widely as to be almost useless, demonstrating once again the notorious unreliability of eyewitness testimony.

Detective Sergeant Wayne Osaka was in charge of the investigation. Tall and rangy, he didn't fit the stereotypical image of the diminutive Japanese American, and perhaps as a form of overcompensation, his manner was anything but deferential. Once Evelyn and Paul were seated in front of his desk in his glass-enclosed office some ninety minutes after the shootings, and he confirmed that neither could identify the gunman, he came straight to the point.

"You two were right in the middle of this God-awful mess. One of you must have some idea who was behind it."

Paul and Evelyn, who had already given preliminary statements at the crime scene, were taken aback by Osaka's bald assertion. "Actually, we don't," Paul said dryly.

"This was an assassination. That much is clear. And by someone who knew what he was doing. Who would want to assassinate your husband, Mrs. McDuffie? And Ms. Gatlin—she wasn't an innocent bystander. This guy had her number, too."

Still shaken, Evelyn spoke haltingly. "I don't know. I just don't know."

"Well, think about it, Mrs. McDuffie."

"That's all I've been doing since it happened," she said wearily.

"Then think harder, because at least one of them rubbed somebody the wrong way—maybe somebody you know."

Paul thought Osaka was being rather harsh. "This is beginning to sound like an interrogation," he said sharply.

"Point taken," Osaka said grudgingly. "Then let me try to get at this another way." He stood and strolled to the other side of the room, folded his arms in front of his chest, and leaned against the wall so that Paul and Evelyn had to turn their heads to see him. "Now, the two of you were on the dance floor together at the time of the shootings. Was that just a coincidence?"

"Are you insinuating—?"

"Evelyn, let me." Paul stood and faced the detective. "Of course, it was a coincidence. As we told the officers at the scene, I hadn't seen Robert *or* Evelyn since college."

Osaka calmly returned to his chair. "Mr. Elliott, please have a seat." Paul sat. "Coincidence or not, there's something else to consider." He paused for a long moment, as though he was still working something out in his mind.

"Well, what is it?" Evelyn finally asked.

"Someone who doesn't know what you look like might have expected you to be sitting at the table with your husband, instead of dancing with Mr. Elliott."

"Meaning the bullet that killed Rachel might have been meant for her," Paul said slowly.

"This can't be happening!" Evelyn gasped. For all Robert's faults, she had once loved him and was genuinely saddened by his death. But now she realized he may have jeopardized, even if unwittingly, her safety and the safety of others around her. She didn't know whether to mourn him or hate him. Her eyes filled with tears and Paul wrapped his arm around her shoulder, the wheels in his mind whirling like a spinning top.

Osaka thought they looked too dazed and dumbfounded to be accomplices in a bizarre double homicide, but he had learned early in his career to take nothing for granted. He expected the unexpected. "Let's get everything out on the table," he said. "First, I want to thank you for allowing us to search your hotel room—that is, the room you shared with Ms. Gatlin. We didn't find anything amiss or helpful, so there's no reason you can't arrange to have her things sent back to Chicago...if that's something you'd like to do."

"Yes...yes. I probably should."

"Now I know you told the other officers that your husband had been tied up with work and had decided at the last minute to join you."

"Yes, that's right."

"But he and Ms. Gatlin didn't switch rooms once he got here."

"No."

"Forgive me for asking, but how were things in your marriage, Mrs. McDuffie?"

She hesitated. "I know this is going to sound terrible, but the truth is..."

"Yes?"

"The truth is it was a disaster. I planned on leaving him and..."

"And?"

"I told him a few minutes before...before he was killed."

"How did he take the news?"

"Fine," she said tersely. "He confessed that he had been seeing Rachel."

"So you didn't know about them before tonight?"

"No."

"Not even a suspicion?"

"No. I knew there were women, but I never suspected Rachel. It was a complete shock."

Osaka paused to try to assemble these new pieces of the puzzle. If these two hadn't seen each other in years (something he'd check out, of course), that ruled out a love triangle. But she could've wanted Robert dead for many reasons. She'd given him one, and maybe there were others. "Was your husband a wealthy man?"

"Hardly. He was in debt up to his eyeballs."

"Insurance policies?"

"Modest. He was a gambler who…who thought he would live forever."

"I see." Osaka would double check, but he suspected she was telling the truth.

"Detective, our marriage was on the rocks, but I would never have done anything to harm Robert," Evelyn said, leaning forward. When she did, Osaka noticed the necklace for the first time. "I wouldn't and I…I couldn't."

"Your necklace, Mrs. McDuffie. A gift from your husband?"

"Yes."

"It looks rather expensive. Do you have any idea how much it's worth?"

"No, I don't."

"When did he give it to you?"

"When we got to Honolulu, as sort of a peace offering. I asked him to return it."

Osaka was puzzled. "If he was having an affair with Ms. Gatlin, why would he give you an expensive gift—especially if he was in so much debt?"

"He said he won some money at the track."

"It doesn't sound like you believed him."

"No, I didn't…Wait a minute. Robert didn't just gamble. He was a *heavy* gambler, and he borrowed a lot of money from a man who's a loan shark, I think. His name is Frank Litvak. Robert told me he paid him back, but that's what he always said."

On its face a large gambling debt didn't add up to a reason to kill two people, unless something more was involved. "Can you think of any other reason Litvak might want to kill your husband—and Ms. Gatlin? Killing them wasn't going to get his money back."

"That's the only thing I can think of."

"Did your husband mention Litvak before you left for the islands or after you got here?"

"No, he didn't."

"What about this man you say—" Osaka corrected himself. "—this man you saw after the shootings?"

"I saw him, too—from behind," Paul said.

"He was definitely carrying a gun. I'm afraid that's mostly what I noticed."

"What kind of gun?"

"I'm no expert. It was a hand gun of some sort."

"Do you remember anything at all about him?"

"He wore sunglasses. He was above average height."

"About Mr. Elliott's height?"

"Yes, about."

"And build?"

"Yes. I only saw him for a few seconds, and then he disappeared. I'd say he was in good condition."

Osaka stood. "Why don't you try to get some rest? I'll make a few calls to see what I can find out about this man Litvak. We'll talk again tomorrow." He paused. "There is one thing I didn't mention. When we searched your room, we found two one-way plane reservations to LA tomorrow, one in Ms. Gatlin's name and one in your husband's."

"So you knew about their affair all along?" Paul said.

"Let's say I had a pretty good idea." He turned to Evelyn. "But I didn't know whether you knew."

"I feel like an even bigger fool now," she said.

"Don't." Paul put his hand on hers.

"I know this has been a difficult night for you," Osaka said. "If you'd like us to notify the next of kin…"

"No," Evelyn said. "I will."

"Use my office. I'll step outside. We'll be in touch." Osaka left.

"You probably want some privacy," Paul said. "I'll be outside, too, if—"

"No." Her eyes welled with tears. "Please stay."

Chapter Twenty-One

Rico lay on his bed fully dressed, hands clasped behind his neck, staring at the ceiling. He had replayed the night's events in his mind over and over, but he couldn't put his finger on something. It wasn't the necklace. However challenging, that problem ultimately could be fixed. Something else had his brain tied up in knots. And until he figured it out, that *couldn't* be fixed—and worse, he could be vulnerable to something he would never see coming.

At a dead end, he turned his thoughts to the necklace. He'd seen it, so no question it had been there. It just hadn't stayed there. He'd searched around the table and was confident he hadn't overlooked it. In the brief period she was out of his sight she must have entrusted it to someone. The logical choice was her tablemate, the woman who had run into him, rushing back from the dance floor—the woman who naturally, but wrongly, feared she would be his next victim. He recalled her face and its familiar look of terror he'd seen so many times before. Could she have been wearing the necklace? He simply didn't know. Even if she wasn't wearing it tonight, she had to know where it was. But it didn't matter. She had to know because if she didn't, he had no idea who did.

Given the couples were together at the luau, chances were good they were staying at the same hotel—his hotel. Undoubtedly the police were questioning the other couple now, but they would be back soon.

Maybe he could intercept them. He decided to go down to the lounge for a drink.

As he turned the doorknob, it hit him! He leaned his back against the door. *The woman racing toward me...the man called her "Evelyn." But I killed Evelyn...How likely was it they were both named Evelyn? Not very. Goddamn it!* So he'd figured it out. But it didn't look like he could fix it.

As he nursed his drink, the TV in the bar confirmed his theory. "...pending notification of next of kin, police haven't revealed the identity of a man and an unrelated woman killed at a luau tonight. The man's wife, also present, escaped injury..."

Rico had another drink. He needed it. It bothered him that he'd killed the wrong woman and he brooded over his blunder. He had called Litvak back and Litvak had assured him that Robert's wife knew what she was doing. He said he had warned her to back off or else. He didn't know whether he believed Litvak or not, but whether he did or he didn't, the woman was playing with fire and she knew it. That was enough for Rico to punch her ticket and not regret it, because she had it coming.

Out of the corner of his eye he saw a solitary couple slow dancing, lost in the moment. The lights were dim and soft music played in the background. He pictured Rachel's face in the crosshairs of the rifle's scope. *This woman didn't have it coming*—at least as far as he knew.

Regrettable as it was that an innocent woman was dead, it had resulted from a serious miscalculation on Rico's part, and that troubled him just as much, if not more. It was the kind of mistake someone in his business couldn't afford to make—the kind he never did, until tonight. Was he slipping? He didn't think so. He hadn't been careless to rely on the purloined photo to identify Evelyn. He'd seen the woman wearing the damn necklace, for Christ's sake, and that, when added to the photo, should have been enough. It was like when Robert got his hands on the necklace in the first place. Sometimes shit happens.

Not only was he not slipping, it looked like he'd reaped a bonus. Robert and the dead woman had to be lovers. Why else was the photo in a duffel bag under the bed? His wife was too upset with him to share a room on a second honeymoon. So who was more likely to be on the phone with Robert bitching to Litvak about giving the necklace back—the wife or the lover? His money was on the lover. Maybe the dead woman was the one Litvak had in mind all along. For a killer with a conscience, it was something.

By the time a police cruiser drew up outside, dropped off Paul and Evelyn, and pulled away, Rico was across the street, hidden in shadows. *Who is this guy?* It wasn't high on his list of questions, but it came to mind again when they arrived together. He followed them in. When they summoned a car at the elevator banks, he was a few yards away almost completely obscured by a large plant, a bamboo palm nearly nine feet tall.

Evelyn's mood swung like a pendulum between sadness and outrage. "I can't stop thinking what a fool I've been. If someone hadn't... if this hadn't happened tonight, they would have been on a plane to LA tomorrow. Probably without a word."

"Evelyn," Paul said, "you have to stop beating yourself up."

"I know, but...can we walk for a little while?"

"Wherever you want."

Elevator cars arrived one after another in quick succession, disgorging streams of people from a meeting in an upstairs ballroom and filling the lobby. Paul and Evelyn headed back outside. When Rico looked again he had lost them in the surging crowd. A moment later he spotted them being swept toward the door. He donned his sunglasses and elbowed his way through the multitude.

A feeling Evelyn couldn't explain caused her to glance over her shoulder. She caught a fleeting glimpse of Rico, well behind her but moving with the crowd in her direction. "Paul," she whispered urgently, "it's him! Behind us."

Paul looked back. "Who?"

"The man from the luau." Evelyn turned, but by then Rico had melted into the host of people. For a moment she wondered whether she'd really seen him.

"Are you sure?"

"No. But what if it *was* him?"

Paul's own words came back to him. *The bullet that killed Rachel might have been meant for her.* They sounded less melodramatic now than they had when he first spoke them. His eyes panned the crowd for anyone that fit the vague description Evelyn had given. No one did. He put his arm around her shoulder and gently guided her toward the door. "Let's walk."

Although it was late, as usual the downtown streets were choked with traffic and the sidewalks packed with shoppers and revelers. They blended into one of the many groups and walked several blocks in silence, ending up on the Kalakaua side of the entrance to the International Marketplace, a cavernous bazaar filled with shops and eateries from the mundane to the exotic. One twisting aisle after another over-flowed with all manner of clothing, fine linens, jewelry, bric-a-brac, souvenirs, and practically anything else. They went in.

Along the streets they'd checked behind them as inconspicuously as possible and seen no one. They continued their vigilance inside, while stopping occasionally, pretending to admire the wares. At the opposite side of the market, they exited on Kuhio Avenue. Compared to Kalakaua it was practically deserted.

Moments later Rico too emerged. Instantly sizing up the situation, it occurred to him that, wittingly or unwittingly, they may have outfoxed him. They had to be looking for a taxi, and he needed to get to them before they found it. Deftly keeping out of sight, he closed the distance between them.

They didn't see him, but as they went down the street Evelyn thought she could sense his presence. She took Paul's arm and forced him to quicken his pace. They saw the headlights of an approaching taxi and hailed it—in vain. It sped past. Rico closed in. Evelyn glanced behind her. He wasn't there. But of course, he was.

Another taxi approached, this time from behind. They flagged it down and it stopped. As they drove off, Evelyn peered out the rear window. Even if she'd been able to locate Rico in the shadows, she couldn't have seen the look of disappointment behind his sunglasses.

Chapter Twenty-Two

Evelyn hadn't laid eyes on Rico since the fleeting encounter in the lobby. But she was convinced, as they rode back to the hotel, that he was the same man she'd almost come face to face with at the luau, that he'd followed them to the International Marketplace without being seen, and that minutes earlier he'd come very close to catching up to them on Kuhio Avenue.

Little by little Paul's initial skepticism faded. He knew Evelyn as a bright and perceptive woman with good instincts. She had always had both feet planted firmly on the ground and was hardly prone to hysteria. Despite the emotional strain of the evening's events, chances were good that her fears were well founded. His challenge was to conceal from her just how much he shared her concern.

Calling Sergeant Osaka crossed his mind, but what could he do? They lacked even a modicum of concrete evidence to support their suspicions. Assuming they could reach him, trying to convince him would waste precious time they didn't have. No, they needed to act quickly, and before the mysterious man with the knack for disappearing into the shadows doubled back to the hotel.

As the taxi approached the hotel, Paul hurriedly described his plan to Evelyn, which he stressed was merely a precaution to allay her fears until they could figure out whether there was truly anything to be fearful about. Evelyn promptly agreed, but sensed more uneasiness in his voice than his reassurances conveyed.

* * *

So adept was Rico at his craft that he knew better than Evelyn herself that for a millisecond she had spotted him in the hotel lobby. He was equally confident that neither she nor the man had seen him between then and the time they entered the taxi on Kuhio Avenue. But he also knew that the one sighting had been enough to arouse their suspicion. They confirmed it with their hurried trek to the marketplace and hasty retreat. They might be anywhere now, but his guess was the hotel. He was reasonably certain the walk to the marketplace hadn't been planned, so they'd probably return to the hotel if only to check out. And if not, he would still have to start his search for them there.

It was a twenty-minute walk to the hotel, unless another taxi happened by. Or he could walk five minutes back to the Kalakaua side of the marketplace, where he could quickly get a taxi. But in that street's heavy traffic, even if the driver turned onto the first side street, he could be another ten minutes away. He started walking and hoped for a passing taxi.

* * *

Paul and Evelyn asked the driver to wait and they hurried to the concierge desk. A tall, blonde man in his early twenties greeted them with an eager smile. Paul didn't give him a chance to ask how he could help. He started with their names and continued from there.

"This is going to sound strange," he said rapidly and precisely, "but we have to change hotels this minute. We need you to pack our luggage and have it delivered to our new hotel. It's an emergency. No time to explain. Here are our key cards and our driver's licenses." He put them on the desk. The concierge looked at him in amazement. "Look at them and satisfy yourself that we are who we say we are." The concierge did as Paul asked. Paul retrieved the licenses, reached in his pocket, peeled off five twenties from his money clip, and handed them to the concierge. "Do you have a list of Honolulu hotels?"

The concierge removed a booklet from a desk drawer behind him and handed it to Paul. "This has a list of all of the hotels in the metropolitan area."

"Perfect." Paul handed him one of his business cards. "Hang onto this. Now if you'll come with us while we check out and run interference, that should just about do it."

As they walked to the front desk, Evelyn remembered Rachel. "My roommate's things are also there. She'll join us later, so pack everything as best you can and we'll sort it out."

The concierge frowned but said nothing. Behind his back Paul winked at Evelyn.

"One last thing," Paul said. "We need to keep this quiet." He handed over five more twenties. "That won't be a problem, will it?"

The concierge beamed. "Certainly not, sir."

* * *

Rico strolled into the lobby and wiped a few uncharacteristic beads of perspiration from his brow with his handkerchief. As a rule, he sweated little, but no taxi had appeared on Kuhio Avenue and he had covered the distance to the hotel at a pace that ranged between a brisk walk and a slow jog. He went to the first white courtesy phone he saw and asked to speak to Evelyn McDuffie. He waited a long moment before the voice came back on the line. She had checked out.

He took out his cell, Googled the airport, and checked for departing flights to the mainland. After confirming there were none that night, he sat in the lobby to consider his options. A few minutes later he paid a visit to the concierge desk.

A man in his early thirties with curly brown hair sat behind the desk. "May I help you, sir?"

"You sure can," Rico began. "Evelyn McDuffie, a friend of mine, had to check out in a hurry a little while ago. She was with another gentleman. Neither one is picking up their cell and I really need to talk to her right now. You didn't happen to give her a hand, did you?"

"I'm sorry, sir, but I've only been here about five minutes."

"What about the concierge you replaced?"

"He'll be back in about an hour."

"It's kind of important. Can you reach him on his cell?

"Afraid not. It's on the fritz. Did you check with the front desk?"

"No, not yet."

"If she left a forwarding address, they'll have it."

"Thanks. I should have thought of that." He had, of course, and he knew there would be no forwarding address.

Chapter Twenty-Three

The concierge accompanied Paul and Evelyn to their waiting taxi. Paul made sure the concierge still had his business card, then told him that once their luggage was loaded into a taxi he should give the card to the driver and ask him to call Paul at the cell number listed there. Paul would tell him where to deliver the luggage.

They took the cab to another hotel about fifteen minutes away, where they switched to a different taxi. Once the new one was some distance from the hotel, Paul and Evelyn went over the list of hotels with the driver and got his suggestion for a modest one, out of the way—one they thought would be far down the list of a pursuer checking off potential hotels where they might be.

The concierge gave a maid and bellman each fifty dollars to pack up the two rooms and take the luggage to a cab. Before going on his break, he gave Paul's card to the bellman, who gave it to the taxi driver, who called Paul as instructed. The plan worked flawlessly.

Their new hotel, off the beaten path, had no concierge and no bellman on duty. Across from the registration desk a large hallway led to the first-floor rooms. An elevator in the lobby led to the second floor. A plain, mid-size conference room was beyond the registration desk, and after that the modest hotel restaurant. Next to that was a door leading outside.

Paul and Evelyn sipped Cokes in the restaurant until their bags arrived. Neither was hungry. Both were exhausted. Without either of them noticing, there appeared to develop an unspoken agreement to resist the urge to talk about their present circumstances. Paul talked about the work piling up in his absence. Evelyn talked about how much she dreaded grading exams. Each awkwardly commiserated with the other.

The maid and bellman had worked quickly, and the luggage arrived in a little over an hour. Paul and Evelyn registered and carried the luggage to their rooms, down the hall near the back of the hotel on the first floor. They were five rooms apart.

"Lock the door and don't let anyone in," Paul said as they stood outside Evelyn's room. "I'll call you in the morning."

"Thanks again," she said and went inside.

Understandably they had difficulty falling asleep. Evelyn was more restless than Paul. At quarter past three he heard a knock on his door.

"Who is it?" he asked groggily, immediately wishing he'd gone quietly to the door and looked through the peephole.

"It's Evelyn," she said self-consciously.

"Is everything all right?"

"Yes. May I come in?"

"Sorry." He jumped out of bed, rubbing his eyes. When he opened the door, half asleep, he realized he was only wearing briefs. He wrapped himself in a towel from the bathroom.

"I'm really sorry," she said.

"That's okay. What's wrong?"

"I finally fell asleep, but I woke up thinking about all the ways someone who was really determined could figure out where we are. I don't think it's safe to stay here."

"Here, sit down." Paul helped her to a chair and sat on the bed as modestly as he could.

She crossed her legs and her robe parted above her knee, revealing several inches of caramel-colored thigh. She didn't notice, but Paul did. "Do you think I'm overreacting?"

"I don't know. We covered our tracks about as well as we could."

"Maybe it's all in my mind."

He noticed the robe again. "I didn't say that. There's a chance some-one has actually been following us, and maybe it's that guy. But I'm not sure what else we can do to throw him off our trail if we haven't already."

"We can change hotels again. This time there won't be anyone between us and the taxi." Paul sighed, not quite imperceptibly. "I'm sorry."

"No. Don't be." He smiled a little. "Sometimes you have to trust your instincts. Have you unpacked yet?"

"Not much. I was too tired to do anything except collapse in bed."

"Then let's leave," he said firmly. "We've taken it this far. If someone really is out there, it won't hurt to put more distance between us. Do you have someplace else in mind?"

"Yes." She stood up, to Paul's immense relief. "Before I came over, I called around."

"I'm impressed. If this is going to make sense, we should leave as soon as possible."

"I'll meet you in the hall in five minutes."

* * *

It was late. Rico had been up all day and he was tired. On most days he was a man of infinite patience, but it was time to find the damn necklace, deal with Evelyn and her companion one way or another (he didn't know how yet), and get the hell out of Dodge. He exited the cab, paid the driver, and surveyed the entrance to the hotel to which Paul and Evelyn had fled.

Half a block from the entrance to the first hotel, he had intercepted the concierge who had helped them. They had a pleasant talk. Rico didn't even have to raise his voice, but then he seldom did, unless for effect. His bearing alone conveyed a seriousness of purpose that left the concierge in no doubt about the difficult straits in which he now found himself. The two hundred dollars Paul had given him, only one hundred of which he still had, now seemed like a paltry sum indeed. He told Rico everything he wanted to know.

In short order Rico tracked the bellman down and, following an equally agreeable conversation with him in an isolated corner of the hotel, the bellman remembered the driver to whom he'd given Paul's business card. He was a regular at the hotel. Once again Rico was luckier than smart. Minutes after this chat the driver happened to return to the hotel in search of another fare. Rico's talk with him was productive.

Now standing in front of the new hotel, Rico examined the surrounding area in detail. Even for the outskirts of the city, it was desolate and poorly lit. *Good thinking. I wouldn't have thought of this place in a million years.* No one was around. He went inside. The lobby was deserted save for the desk clerk, a solidly built man of about fifty with a mop of red hair and a ruddy complexion, who was reading a magazine and listening to the radio.

Rico adjusted his sunglasses and strode to the desk, removing his .45 as he went. Before the clerk knew he was there, the gun barrel was against his forehead. Appropriately stunned, the man shut his eyes and, like others before him, later would remember virtually nothing about Rico except the dark glasses and very large gun.

"Is anybody else here besides you?" Rico demanded.

The man was too terrified to speak. It was a familiar reaction.

"I said is anybody else here?" Rico pressed, each syllable distinct.

"N-no, just me."

"Take me to Evelyn McDuffie's room."

"Can I look at the register?" the clerk stammered.

"Hurry up." The man did. "Now get me the key and start walking."

Rico shifted the .45 to his side and followed the clerk to Evelyn's room. He told the man to lie face down on the hall floor, hands behind his head and eyes closed. Rico eased the key card into the lock and turned the doorknob. He expected to find the door chained from the inside and to have to kick it free, but when he pushed the door, it swung open, revealing lights on in both the bedroom and the bathroom. Maybe that meant she didn't care about conserving electricity. He figured it meant she'd left in a hurry.

Rico walked in. The room and bathroom were empty, as was the closet. No hint that anybody would be returning. Maybe, he thought, she'd joined her companion in another room. He walked back to the hall and stood spread-eagle over the desk clerk's downturned head.

"Get up and keep your face pointed away from me." After the man was on his feet, Rico looked down the hall in both directions and saw no one. "This woman checked in with a man. What room is he in?"

The desk clerk was trembling and answered haltingly. "I don't know. I just came on duty a few minutes ago."

"Take a walk back to the desk. Keep your eyes straight ahead and walk naturally. If we run into anybody, don't say a word. I'll take care of it." They didn't see anyone.

When they reached the desk, Rico grabbed the register and slid it to the clerk. "Find her name and tell me who else checked in at the same time."

"Paul Elliott. But...but...they both checked out twenty minutes ago."

"Shit! Why didn't you tell me that before?" But he already knew.

"I was so nervous...I...I just noticed it. I'm sorry."

Maybe I should change my approach, he mused.

It was time to repeat the exercise he'd gone through with the cabbie whose taxi he'd commandeered to get to the luau. It always worked. Once, out of curiosity, after he had ordered a man to lie on the ground in an alley and not to get up for an hour, he had come back fifty-five minutes later to see if he was still there. He was, although no longer prone. He sat with his back against a building, staring at his watch.

He rattled off instructions to the desk clerk. "Get back on the floor, face down behind the counter and don't move for thirty minutes. And I mean don't move. I may come back, and if I do I want to find you right there."

Without a word the man lay down as directed, resolved to wait a full hour for good measure before going home to change his soiled pants.

Chapter Twenty-Four

Osaka made some calls to Chicago. Paul and Evelyn were upstanding citizens. Litvak was, of course, another matter.

Years ago, he'd hijacked a truckload of cigarettes and done time at Joliet. His was a familiar story. The stretch in prison only taught him how to become a more successful criminal. He moved on to illegal gambling, loan sharking, extortion, high-end burglary, and when necessary, murder, although he hadn't committed one himself in more than a dozen years. He could hire plenty of others to handle such details.

Although the Chicago police knew about his illicit activities, they hadn't been able to pin anything on him since his release from prison. They'd come close once, about three years before. The men who worked for Litvak were unusually loyal, both because they were well paid for their work and because, with one notable exception, they feared him. And with good reason. So the police couldn't get any of them to flip, until the day Lonnie Blakemore fell into their laps.

Lonnie robbed a small neighborhood bank to pay off some gambling debts and got careless. He didn't check the gas gauge in the getaway car he'd stolen minutes before entering the bank, and it ran out of gas less than a mile away. The police sealed off the area and found him hiding under a bridge. When an alert detective recognized him as one of the men on Litvak's payroll, he hid the arrest from the press and arranged with the state's attorney to offer him a deal. It was an agonizing decision for Lonnie but, if he balked, with his record he faced up to twenty-five years. He took the deal.

He was to set up a meeting with Litvak the next day and wear a wire. But somebody who knew Lonnie saw him arrested and told another of Litvak's henchmen, who was surprised to see Lonnie on the street the next day since he knew he couldn't make bail. The information got to Litvak, whose source inside the police department confirmed the arrest but could find neither a record of it nor why Lonnie was released, although he had his suspicions.

To Litvak it added up to just one thing.

Lonnie never made it to the meeting. His body, dismembered and buried in a vacant field, was never found.

After his Chicago PD briefing, Osaka knew Litvak was capable of reaching across the ocean and killing two people. But what was his motive? He'd need a second conversation with Evelyn. He dialed the number of the hotel she'd given him, but she and Paul had checked out. He scratched his head and asked to be connected to the night manager.

"This is Detective Sergeant Osaka of the Honolulu Police Department. Can you tell me when Evelyn McDuffie and Paul Elliott checked out of your hotel and where they went?"

"I'm sorry, sir," the manager said crisply. "I don't mean to be difficult, but if you are a police officer I'm sure you understand that I have no way of verifying it. Without some identification I can't release that information to you."

Osaka was livid. "Listen, you little prick. I don't have time for this bullshit. I want that information and I want it now. Do I make myself clear?"

The manager held his ground. "I'm sorry, sir, but I cannot release that information."

Osaka took a slow breath. The manager was right. "I apologize. I shouldn't have lost my temper. You're right. Here is the number for the Honolulu Police Department." He gave it. "After we hang up, please call it and ask for Detective Sergeant Osaka. Is that fair?"

"I didn't mean to be difficult," the manager said apologetically, "but I—"

"I know, I know. Just call that number as soon as we hang up, okay?"

The manager called back and the call was put through.

"Detective Sergeant Osaka."

"I'm terribly sorry."

"Please, you don't have to apologize. You did the right thing. The next time someone calls, maybe he won't be a cop. Now, can you tell me when they left and where they went?"

The manager could only tell him when they'd checked out.

"Great," Osaka said, exasperated.

* * *

As Evelyn and Paul approached the registration desk at the third hotel, she gently touched his elbow.

Paul yawned involuntarily. "Is everything all right?"

"Yes…" She hesitated a moment, not meeting his gaze.

"Are you sure?"

"Listen. Under the circumstances, I don't know why I'm feeling so coy about this, but would you mind if we shared a room? I'm terrified."

"Is that all? I almost suggested it myself. I'm glad you did."

"Good! Now maybe I can get some sleep. I don't think I could have otherwise."

"A perfect gentleman, cross my heart." Paul drew a cross on his chest with a forefinger.

She laughed softly and felt better. "Thanks."

* * *

Evelyn was right. Under the circumstances neither of them should have felt awkward. But despite the circumstances, Paul's mind was as much on Evelyn as it was on the killer they had presumably been eluding all evening and who could be closing in on them that very minute.

The little episode at the other hotel when he couldn't keep his eyes off her shapely thigh proved that. So he slept fitfully, uncomfortable with the thought of a beautiful woman asleep in a bed a few feet from his, a woman who had been the object of his college fantasies and whose vulnerability somehow made her more desirable now than ever. He felt guilty because he didn't care that her philandering husband had been murdered a few hours earlier. It engendered in him a powerful urge to protect her, but it did nothing to dampen his desire to take her in his arms and escape the horror of that night in her embrace.

She had gone into the bathroom first to get ready for bed and a few minutes later had emerged wearing a short silk robe. While he sat on his bed, they exchanged smiles as she walked past him to her bed, at which point he rose to take his turn in the bathroom. By the time he came out, she was already under the covers. Although her back was facing him, she appeared to be fast asleep. He turned out the light and climbed into bed.

"Good night," she said softly.

"Good night."

* * *

Paul guessed that he'd slept for perhaps an hour. At times he could hear Evelyn tossing and turning as well. Now he lay awake thinking about all that had transpired the night before. *Are we really on the run and being pursued by a murderer for who knows what reason?* But even if that weren't true, there surely had been two murders. *Maybe it was a mistake not to call the police. But it's too late to worry about that now. Concentrate on the future. We'll call Osaka first thing. Maybe something turned up last night. Give him a chance to do his job before going off on some frolic of your own.*

As he listened to Evelyn's steady breathing, thoughts of her again intruded. So much had happened so quickly that he scarcely understood how she had so thoroughly worked herself into his psyche. He thought about JoAnne and re-affirmed that he was finally at peace with her death and that he was free to move on. Then he kicked himself. Robert had been a miserable excuse for a human being, but still he and Rachel—no prize either—had been brutally murdered. *Paul, get a grip.*

She stirred a little and he turned his back to her so that he couldn't see the outline of her body beneath the covers. He forced himself to think about the problems at hand. The weight of what was happening to them pressed hard against his chest and he felt it tighten. *What if Evelyn was right?* They might both be killed. He realized it now, as though for the first time.

Evelyn got out of bed, threw on her robe, walked past his bed, and headed toward the bathroom, unaware that he was awake. He turned just enough to look in her direction. She stopped at the luggage stand near the door and leaned over to find her toilet bag and a change of clothes. The tantalizingly short robe barely reached below her hips. How stunning she was, Paul thought. He turned over on his other side.

When she heard him change positions, she stood up from searching her luggage and turned to face him. "Are you awake?"

"Yes." He still had his back to her.

"For very long?"

"Only a few seconds."

"You can turn around now."

He propped himself up on his elbows and rubbed his eyes. "Did you sleep any better?"

"Yes. I woke up a couple of times, but I was able to get back to sleep. How about you?"

"The same," he lied. Then their eyes met and, for an awkward moment, neither spoke. "I guess we should call that police detective."

She smiled and he did, too. "Definitely. But let me get showered and dressed first."

The moment passed. She went into the bathroom and Paul got up, wrapped a towel around himself, and waited his turn.

Chapter Twenty-Five

Osaka was relieved to hear Evelyn's voice on the other end of the line. He hadn't known whether she and Paul were dead or alive. He listened patiently to her breathless description of the previous night, interrupting only to ask for clarification, or to say, "I see" or "Go on," all of which struck Evelyn as peculiar in light of what she was saying.

What she didn't know was that (other than the fact they were safe) Osaka had pieced together much of what had happened and why. After learning that she and Paul checked out, he went to the hotel to see what he could find out. A clerk at the front desk told him Evelyn and Paul didn't have their luggage, and later she saw the bellman, unaccompanied by hotel guests, taking luggage to a taxi. Neither event alone was particularly unusual, but she wondered whether perhaps they were related.

Osaka tracked down the bellman and maid, still on duty. They couldn't remember the name on Paul's card, but it had read "attorney at law." They described the clothing in the two rooms, including the two sets of toiletries belonging to the woman. Osaka was sure it was Paul and Evelyn. The bellman knew the taxi driver's first name, but not whether he'd be returning to the hotel for additional fares. Osaka waited an hour with no luck. He left his card but didn't receive a call back.

The concierge wasn't forthcoming until Osaka said he'd already spoken to the maid and bellman. That seemed to jar his memory. He said Paul and Evelyn asked for his help to check out quickly and deliver their luggage to another hotel.

"Did that seem strange to you?" Osaka asked.

"Not really. You'd be surprised at some of the requests we get." Then he related his conversation with a well-built man with dark hair who wore sunglasses and said he was anxious to get in touch with two friends but hadn't been able to reach them on their cells. He didn't tell Osaka he hadn't bought that story. Nor did he say that when he told the man he couldn't help him, without brandishing a weapon or even raising his voice the man had frightened him more than anyone in his life. He did tell Osaka that after the man explained how urgently he needed to reach Paul and Evelyn, he'd bent the rules and put him in contact with the bellman, to whom he'd given Paul's business card.

"And giving this card to the cabbie didn't strike you as odd either, I take it?"

"No, it didn't," the concierge said, straight-faced.

"Well, son, it sounds to me like these two people were trying to stay one step ahead of someone. Didn't you think you might be leading this man right to them?"

"That…that didn't occur to me. And their friend…well, he was so insistent."

"Did this man threaten you?"

"No, not at all. I would have said something if he had."

Osaka didn't buy it. But plainly the concierge was still scared to death and, in any event, other than the description he'd given of Rico, he couldn't add anything to what the bellman and maid had told him. "Is that the best description you can give me?"

"He met me outside just before I came in and there wasn't a lot of light where we were standing," the concierge said resolutely. "Sorry, but that's the best I can do."

"I'll bet."

As he turned to leave, the clerk he'd interviewed at the front desk motioned him over. "There's a rumor that the two people killed at the luau were guests here…"

He gave her the stock reply. "I'm sorry, but I can't confirm that one way or the other until we notify next of kin." Clearly, she wanted to say something, and it could be helpful. He didn't want to dissuade her by being too dismissive. He added amiably, "I'm sure you understand."

By the time she finished speaking to Osaka, he had his motive.

Evelyn finished describing their ordeal.

"Did either of you actually see this man?" Osaka asked.

"Don't tell me you still don't believe us!"

"As a matter of fact, I do."

"You do?"

"Yes. Right now, the man is a ghost. I just want to know if somebody can give me a description of him I can work with, and from what I'm hearing you still can't."

"Nothing beyond what I already told you."

"Would it be much of an imposition for you and Mr. Elliott to come back down to the station for a few minutes this morning?"

"No, of course not. Do you think you can find this man?"

"We'll do our best, but I won't lie to you. It's not going to be easy. Will you bring the ruby necklace you were wearing last night? I'd like to have someone take a look at it, if that's okay."

"You think it's involved in all this?"

"Let's take a look at it first. We'll have a better idea then."

"What time would you like us to be there?"

"Could you be here in an hour?"

Evelyn asked Paul. He was certain they hadn't been followed to this hotel, so he suggested an hour and a half to give them time to grab breakfast.

Osaka called one of his officers. "Tell Zaremba we'll need him in an hour and a half."

Paul and Evelyn ordered breakfast in the hotel restaurant.

"I want to thank you again," she said.

"No more thank-yous," Paul said firmly.

"But I still feel so…presumptuous about getting you involved in all this."

"We're in this together. We *did* just spend the night together." They smiled.

"It helps to smile a little. This is such a nightmare." Her voice cracked and her eyes became a stream of tears. She looked out the window. "Excuse me. It's so unreal. I still can't believe everything that's happened."

Paul felt helpless. "Hey, hang in there. You're doing great. And if you feel like crying, go ahead." He reached across the table and gently took her hands in his. She composed herself and the tears subsided. "Feel a little better?"

"It's so odd. I should be in mourning." She looked down at her outfit. She wore sandals without stockings, a short-sleeved blouse, and a print skirt a few inches above the knee.

Paul thought again how beautiful she looked. "I'm sure anybody who knew what was going on would understand. It's not like you packed with this in mind."

"It's not only that. I...I wonder whether I did everything I could."

One reason she'd tossed and turned much of the previous night was that she'd spent hours recounting her wasted years with Robert. Her parents had been right about him. He was the charming Lothario they said he was. Still, nobody is all bad, and he had his moments—like early in their marriage when she had pneumonia and he sat by her bed patiently nursing her back to health. For all his faults, he hadn't deserved to die, certainly not like this.

And what of her role in their marriage? All her efforts to reform him had failed, which made her question whether she might have changed something about herself. She had to admit that she wasn't always as supportive of his ambitions and dreams as she might have been. But that surely didn't excuse his many transgressions. Nevertheless, the question lingered.

"Evelyn, you shouldn't blame yourself for any of this," Paul said. "You're really under a lot of pressure—"

"I know. I can't help it."

"Listen, it's one thing to feel sorry that he's dead, but there's no reason to feel guilty about what happened to your marriage. That was his fault, not yours."

She closed her eyes, exhausted and frightened. But Paul was such a comfort. "Are you sure you're a lawyer and not a therapist?" They smiled again.

Chapter Twenty-Six

They arrived at the police station a few minutes early and were taken to a small, windowless room with a plain wooden table and four chairs in the center. Osaka sat there.

"Thanks for coming," he said, rising to shake hands.

"Are we being interrogated?" Paul asked.

"No, no, of course not. Didn't Mrs. McDuffie tell you? We had some logistical problems this morning I thought would be straightened out by now—too many people and too few places to talk—and this room was the only one available." He motioned to the table. "Please, have a seat." Osaka explained how he'd gone to the hotel the night before and what he'd learned. "And your scheme was brilliant! My compliments on your choice of hotels, too. *I* wouldn't have looked for you there. Unfortunately, our man was one step ahead of you. The bellman only knew the first name of your cabbie, and I had no idea how to locate him. Maybe it was just dumb luck, but the guy we're after was a better detective than I was. He managed to be there when the cabbie came back and the bellman pointed him out."

"You mean he found out where we'd gone?" Evelyn asked.

"Just like that. Lucky for you—and me, too—he got there just after you left, which was quick thinking on your part. My compliments again."

"Wait a minute," Paul said. "How did you know he got there right after we left?"

"Because the desk clerk's boss called it in this morning."

"Was his description any better than mine?" Evelyn asked.

"Depressingly similar, but he did recall dark hair. Does that ring a bell?"

"That sounds right, but I'm not sure."

"Anyway," Osaka resumed, frustrated, "he must've given up after the second hotel."

"For now, at least."

"Let's not be too pessimistic," Paul said. "Maybe this is the last we've heard of this character." But he didn't really believe that, even as he looked to Osaka for support, insincere as it would be. Evelyn saw right through it.

"I appreciate what you're trying to do, Paul, but this man has gone to a lot of trouble to get to me. Nothing he's done so far has given us any reason to think he won't continue."

"It's *us* he's been after, Evelyn. We're still in this together."

"The truth is we don't know how badly he wants to catch up with either of you," Osaka said. "But I do know why. I asked you to bring that necklace with you for a reason."

Evelyn removed it from her purse and passed it across the table. Osaka examined it in the light from the ceiling fixture. It didn't look any less valuable today than it had the night before when he first spied it around her neck. "As I mentioned on the phone, I'm going to have somebody who knows more about these things look at this."

"Please," Evelyn said.

"Last night as I was about to leave the hotel, a desk clerk called me over. All the clerks on duty yesterday had been talking about this case since they heard the news on TV. They figured out that your husband and Ms. Gatlin were the victims and were comparing notes about them. Someone remembered that your husband called from his room earlier that evening asking whether you'd left an expensive necklace he'd just bought for you in the safe. They told him you hadn't, and it didn't raise any red flags until they wondered later why you and he were staying in separate rooms, especially after he'd just bought you an expensive necklace. Still later, and this is the kicker, one of the clerks said she was certain that your husband, whom she recognized because he'd flirted with her, was already on the bus to the luau when he was supposedly upstairs calling from his room and asking about the necklace."

"It was him," Evelyn said.

"Yes, and you were right about one thing. He *has* gone to a lot of trouble—to get this." Osaka held up the necklace.

"That explains Rachel's reaction at the luau," Paul said.

"What do you mean?"

"Robert was drunk," Evelyn said. "He tried to say something about the necklace and Rachel went ballistic."

"Any idea what he had in mind?"

"No," Evelyn said. "I never even wanted it. I just took it back from Rachel because I was so upset with Robert. I never would have kept it."

"Maybe they knew that, too," Paul said.

"I still haven't connected our man and Litvak, but Litvak is the most likely link we've got to this whole mess," Osaka said. "My guess is he sent the killer here to collect the necklace. I think somehow your husband got his hands on it and skipped town with this guy on his heels."

"That would explain his last-minute change of plans," Evelyn said.

"Perversely, it all seems to make sense," Paul said.

"Well, there's at least one other loose end," Osaka said. "I still haven't figured out why he thought the two murders last night would lead him to the necklace since you had it all along, Mrs. McDuffie. Unless..."

"I didn't," Evelyn said. "I let Rachel try it on earlier but I took—she gave it back to me just before she was killed."

"He confused the two of you," Osaka said.

"And he must have been trying to find the necklace when Evelyn and I saw him near the bodies," Paul said.

"It fits," Osaka said. "They were both killed with a single shot from long range and died instantly. I don't think the killer needed to make sure they were dead."

Silence filled the room as Paul and Evelyn digested all that had been said. After a few seconds, Osaka continued. "Let's fill in the last piece of the puzzle." He picked up the phone and dialed. "Bring Mr. Zaremba in."

"Who is he?" Paul asked.

"A gemologist." An officer appeared at the door with a distinguished-looking man of about sixty, as thin as a rail with a neatly trimmed salt-and-pepper goatee and horn-rimmed glasses. "Here is the necklace I mentioned on the phone this morning, Mr. Zaremba. Would you mind taking a look at it?"

"Certainly." He took the necklace in his hands with relish. "This is extraordinary!" He removed a loupe from the inside pocket of his jacket, placed the necklace under it, and examined it closely. "Extraordinary! Pigeon-blood red, definitely."

"What do you mean?" Osaka said.

"May I?" Zaremba said, pointing to an empty chair.

"Of course."

Zaremba took a seat at the table and, like a college professor giving a lecture without notes, launched into a lengthy disquisition on the origin, characteristics, significance, and value of pigeon-blood red rubies.

"'Pigeon-blood red' was a phrase coined by Indian gem dealers centuries ago. It's the most desirable color a ruby can have. In legend it's said to replicate the hue of the first two drops of blood that trickle from the nostrils of a freshly killed pigeon.

"Throughout history, rubies, the name of which comes from the Latin *ruber* for red, have been known as the king of gemstones. In Sanskrit the ruby is called 'the king of precious stones.' Of the four traditional ones—rubies, sapphires, emeralds, and diamonds—rubies occur most frequently in the English translation of the Bible. I'm sure you're familiar with 'the price of wisdom is beyond rubies,' a verse from Job, or 'a virtuous wife is worth more than rubies,' from Proverbs."

"Of course," Evelyn said. Paul and Osaka looked at each other quizzically.

"Go on," Osaka said.

"Only diamonds are harder, measuring 10.0 on the Mohs scale of mineral hardness, whereas rubies measure 9.0. With the exception of red diamonds, carat for carat rubies are the highest-priced colored gemstones, and pigeon-blood red rubies, the highest quality natural rubies, are rarer and more valuable than comparable colorless diamonds. Until recently, the record sum paid for a single 38.12-carat ruby was $5.86 million in 2006, while the record amount paid per carat was a spectacular $421,981 in the same year for an 8.62 carat gem known as the Graff Ruby. However, in May of 2015 the Sunrise Ruby, weighing 25.59 carats, was sold at Sotheby's Auction House in Geneva for a staggering 28.25 million Swiss francs, which is equivalent to about the same amount in US dollars at current exchange rates. That exceeds one million dollars per carat, more than doubling the previous record.

"Traditionally the source of the world's finest and most prized rubies, like these, has been the Mogok Stone Tract, sometimes called the Valley of Rubies, an area covering about four hundred square miles north of Mandalay in Myanmar. Burma, if you prefer. This region produces, in quantities that are rapidly dwindling, pigeon-blood red rubies that are completely natural, the most valuable kind. Unlike rubies of lesser quality, natural ones need not be treated by heat, lasers, or fillers to enhance their color and clarity. They are, however, extremely rare, and fewer than one in twenty thousand qualifies as pigeon-blood red.

"All rubies unearthed in Myanmar belong to the state and are supposed to be transported to Rangoon to be sold. In actuality, most are smuggled into Bangkok, and although there is no way to be certain, that was the likely path traveled by the sixteen color-matched rubies that make up this necklace."

"What are they worth?" Osaka asked.

"I can't say. How much would a willing buyer pay? The prices I just quoted to you represent the known outer limits."

"Could these be worth that much?"

"They are remarkable stones." Zaremba smiled almost beatifically.

"Any questions?" Osaka asked Paul and Evelyn.

"Is there any way to know who owns them?" Paul asked.

"No," Zaremba said. "Some are in museums. Some are in private collections we know about. Others, we just don't know—until they surface, like these did."

"I checked the wire for a stolen necklace fitting this description, and for individual rubies as well," Osaka said. "I came up empty."

"So if they were stolen, the owner hasn't reported them?" Paul asked.

"At least not yet." Osaka raised an eyebrow to solicit additional questions. Hearing none, he stood. "Mr. Zaremba, thank you for your help. We'll be in touch if we need anything further." The gemologist left, and Osaka asked, "Did that surprise you as much as it did me?"

"Shock would be a better word," Evelyn said.

"I'll tell you another one. Stumped. That's what I am," Osaka said.

"I think you had it figured out pretty well," Paul said. "But where does it leave us?"

"That's what I mean. What do you folks intend to do now?"

"We have tickets on a flight to Chicago this afternoon. I don't know whether anyone is still stalking us, but we'd both feel safer in our own territory. No offense."

"None taken."

"It would have been better to stay until arrangements were made for Robert and Rachel," Evelyn said. "But that doesn't make sense now, with all that's happened. We can handle those details by phone and e-mail, can't we?"

"Of course."

"Then, I guess that's about it, except..." Paul said.

"The necklace." Osaka strode to the other side of the room and turned to face them. "As I said, it's not officially missing. Although I'll bet dollars to donuts Litvak is up to his eyeballs in this, I don't know for sure and I can't prove it. I also don't know how your husband got his mitts on it, but it's a cinch he didn't buy it and nobody gave it to him as a present. Since I can't prove he stole it, or that anybody else did, there's no reason for us to keep it unless you want us to. You can do what you want with it, including giving it back to Litvak." He returned to the table and stood behind his chair to await their reactions.

"Are you serious?" Evelyn said. "You're suggesting approaching Litvak to give it back?"

"Or you could keep it. Until someone says otherwise, it does belong to you."

"For now," Paul said.

"It's a lot of money, but it's not mine to keep," Evelyn said. "I have a strong feeling somebody out there isn't going to rest until he gets it back."

"Then as I see it, you have two choices," Osaka said. "You could leave it with us or with the Chicago police, and maybe the owner will eventually claim it. Or you could arrange to meet with Litvak and wear a wire. I can set it up with Chicago."

"That could be dangerous," Paul said.

"Yeah, it could."

* * *

Later that day, a detective walked into Osaka's office.

"There's a guy downstairs who says his cab was hijacked to that luau last night where the murders took place. The hijacker forced him into the trunk until this morning. He heard the shots and commotion from the trunk and put two and two together when he heard the news this morning. All he remembers is the guy had dark curly hair, large sunglasses, and a huge automatic. That's it."

"Well, well, well," Osaka said. "So now not only do we know that this tall, well-built, athletic man has dark hair, we also know that it's curly."

Then something occurred to him and he kicked himself for not having thought of it earlier. He picked up the phone to dial but thought better of it and rushed to his car. When he reached the hotel, he walked briskly to the front desk. Before the clerk could open his mouth, Osaka flashed his badge. "I need to see your surveillance tapes for the last twenty-four hours."

"I'm sorry," the desk clerk stammered, "but there aren't any. The system has been down for the last couple of days. They had to locate a special part. They're working on it now."

"It figures," Osaka muttered as he turned and walked away.

Part Three

Chapter Twenty-Seven

It was a smooth flight and the plane landed on time. It felt good to be home. As the plane taxied to a stop, Rico looked out the window and thought of Jean. He hadn't called her or allowed her to call him since he left. Hearing her voice would have been a distraction he didn't need. His mind drifted to his solitary jog on the beach in Honolulu and the idyllic view of the ocean from his hotel room that had so captivated him, and he pictured Jean beside him.

He disembarked and, as he made his way from one concourse to the next to retrieve his luggage, he punched in Jean's number on his cell. To her dismay, her anger had morphed into mere annoyance, and even that dissolved when she heard his voice. "Are you all right?" she asked, trying not to sound as happy and relieved as she actually was.

"Great. I missed you."

"You did?" she said, surprised not that he'd missed her but that he'd acknowledged it.

"Sure."

"Well, you should have."

"And what about you?"

"I'm just glad you're okay."

"Is that all?"

"You know I missed you, too. In spite of everything, I did."

"You know where I was?"

"Rico, you never—"

"I was in Honolulu, and you know what? It was peaceful. It was beautiful. Ever been there?"

"No, but I've always dreamed—"

"Would you like to go?"

"Rico, I'd love to."

"Good. I have a few things to clean up here, but after that we'll go."

Jean felt like she was dreaming and she hesitated to say anything that would wake her. But she couldn't resist. "A few things?" She knew she would not press it beyond that.

Rico had already opened up much more than usual, so he retreated to familiar territory. "Just a piece of business," he said gently but firmly. "It won't take long." He didn't think it would.

* * *

Jean was as happy as she'd been in years. So she was upset with herself when she was unable to stop herself from searching the Internet, where she found news of two unexplained murders at a luau in Honolulu. After she had a chance to think about it, she told herself that murders occur somewhere every day, and that just because two people happened to get themselves killed when Rico was in town didn't mean he had anything to do with it. That was only logical, wasn't it?

She had known Rico for a few years. She was at a lively bar on Rush Street celebrating a girlfriend's birthday along with a handful of other women when Rico and Jerry walked in. Jerry saw her first. She was so gorgeous his mouth watered. Obviously, she was way out of his league, so he didn't think much of his chances. That didn't stop him, though. She was sitting at a table with three other women when he strolled over, introduced himself, and asked to buy her a drink.

Jean hesitated. She already saw too much of men, and that night she just wanted to let her hair down a little and relax with her friends. But when she politely declined, her tablemates gently nudged her to accept. She hadn't noticed Rico when he and Jerry came in, but they had. With her out of the way, the odds improved for one of them to reel

Rico in. She thought about it. Jerry wasn't a bad-looking guy. Maybe they could have a few laughs. She accepted his offer. As soon as she did, two of the other women stood almost simultaneously. The one who was closer to Rico's table got there first, leaving her friend standing with her hands on her hips, and asked whether she could join him. He said, "Why not?"

Meanwhile, as Jerry and Jean made their way to a separate table, she made eye contact with Rico. She was impressed. He was, too. Her face showed it. His didn't. Jerry pulled a chair out for her. She demurely suggested another one and he obliged with a grin that he wished he could take back when he realized she had positioned herself so that she faced Rico. Jerry smiled to himself and gamely shook his head. After all, it wasn't like it was the first time this had happened.

"Come on," Jerry said, taking Jean's hand and standing.

"What?" she said, surprised.

"Come on," he repeated. She stood and he led her to Rico's table. "Rico, this is Jean," he said.

"Jerry, this is Connie," Rico said.

"Mind if we join you?"

"Please," Rico said.

Connie folded her arms across her chest and glanced across the room at her girlfriends, who acknowledged her with a tip of their drinks. It wasn't like it was the first time this had happened to them either.

After that, Jean and Rico and Jerry and Connie exchanged small talk for several minutes. Jean did try, but she couldn't keep her eyes off Rico. After a while she gave up. Connie tried to compete, but in short order she gave up, too. She would have preferred Rico but Jerry would do. She sighed audibly. That was Rico's cue.

"Jerry, Connie, you don't mind, do you?" He was almost asking permission but not quite.

Connie forced a smile. Jerry said, "Connie?"

"Sure, why not?" she said.

"Jean?" Rico said. And they both stood and left the bar.

They saw each other at least every week after that and sometimes two or three times a week. He didn't have to tell her what he did for a living. She knew he wasn't a policeman or anything like one. Yet he carried his .45 with him everywhere and never tried to hide it from her. He never took it out in front of her but she could feel it when they embraced, and if she looked carefully, she could see the bulge under his jacket. One day she decided to mention it. They were strolling through the park one afternoon when he stopped to tie a shoelace, and she saw the gun peeking out of his shoulder holster. When he straightened up, he asked casually, "Does that bother you?"

"How did you know?" she asked.

"Know what?"

"That I was finally going to say something about it."

"I had a hunch."

"Didn't you wonder why I didn't say anything before now?"

"I figured you'd get around to it."

She hesitated a second and looked directly in his eyes. "So why do you carry it?"

He returned her gaze and held it. "It's a cold world out there. Sometimes I have to protect myself or people I work for. And sometimes other people have to protect themselves from me—or at least, try." He patted the bulge in his jacket. "Either case, this comes in handy."

Jean looked away. "I see…" she said, not surprised but nevertheless a little sad. "I guess that answers my question."

Rico reached out and gently took her cheek in his hand and turned her face to him. "Look, this is the business I'm in, Jean, but I'll tell you one more thing and you can take it or leave it. So far, I never shot anyone who didn't have it coming."

So that was that, she thought. At least he was honest. That counted for something. Besides, she wasn't about to start a long-term relationship with the man and wasn't in a position to do so even if she wanted to. Most women in her line of work couldn't hope for such things. Enjoy it while it lasts, she told herself, and that's what she intended to do.

They continued their walk in silence.

A few weeks later she and her ex-husband got into a heated argument, and he got drunk and tried to force his way into her apartment. She pointedly didn't tell Rico, but her girlfriend told Jerry, who mentioned it to Rico. Rico knew he was a bully and a loudmouth but not really dangerous. So there was no reason for him to die. Still, such conduct ought to be discouraged since one never really knew for sure what a man might do in the midst of a drunken rage. The next time Jean saw her ex-husband, his arm was in a cast. For some reason he was unusually civil and a perfect gentlemen in his dealings with her from then on. But he refused to discuss how he broke his arm.

Rico didn't ask Jean what she did for a living and she didn't volunteer for almost a month. It took her that long to summon the courage to tell him.

Then one night as they were driving to her apartment after seeing a movie, she said glumly, "I have something to tell you."

"Shoot."

"It's about my...job. You've never asked. Aren't you curious?"

"I didn't have to ask," he said impassively.

"You didn't?"

"I know," he said.

"You do?"

"Yeah."

"Who told you?"

"No one."

"How long have you known?"

"It took me about a week to figure it out."

"A week?" She was shocked. He had known that long and hadn't said a word.

"Yeah. More or less."

"And it doesn't matter?" Then she stopped herself. Was she presuming too much? "Or does it?"

"No."

"But how do you *feel* about it?"

"How do you feel about what I do?"

"Well…it doesn't change the way I feel about *you.*"

"See, that was simple."

"But this is different—isn't it?"

"A job is a job. It's not who you are."

She didn't know what to say to that and so she didn't say anything. But she didn't need to. Rico's comment said it all. And it explained a lot about their relationship.

Still, there was a lot to say. It just wasn't said that night.

Hers was a complicated story. She and her three younger sisters had been raised by their mother after their father skidded off a rain-slicked highway into a tree and killed himself when she was thirteen. He was a department store salesman with no life insurance. Jean was a good student and wanted to go to college. Instead, when she graduated from high school, she got a job waiting tables to augment her mother's earnings as a drug store cashier.

Over time the caliber of restaurants improved along with the size of her tips, but her dismal luck with men stayed the same. She eventually married a man who worked as a meat distributor for one of the restaurants where she waited tables. He ate there from time to time, always with a different woman. That should have told her something. He promised to take her away from "all this," but all she got was lonely nights when he was away on his frequent sales trips and verbal abuse when he was home.

Slowly, the constant haranguing took its toll, gradually affecting her already fragile self-esteem. Men (and women) had always told her how attractive she was. Yet she somehow always seemed to end up in destructive relationships. She eventually came to believe that her body was her sole attribute. Her tips, for instance, were perennially higher than anyone else's. It wasn't hard for her to figure out why. The men she knew all seemed to want only one thing. Well, why not make them pay for it? After six months, she got a divorce, and did that just that.

* * *

Now that Rico had left the islands and could do nothing more for the time being, he felt no urgency to deliver that news to Litvak, who would disagree. But so be it.

Litvak had called several times after Rico had distinctly told him not to, so he ignored the calls. In fact, one of them came through as Rico was closing in on Paul and Evelyn outside the International Marketplace. The phone was on vibrate, but it annoyed him that Litvak had called and he turned it off after that.

Rico had returned to his hotel and checked out immediately after missing the pair at the second hotel. There wasn't even a cab stand at that hotel, and he knew that locating the driver who'd picked up Evelyn and Paul would take a miracle. He had had his one stroke of luck that night and he wasn't due for another one. He went directly to the airport. No flights to Chicago were available until mid-afternoon, but the first one had an available seat. He took out his dog-eared copy of *From Here to Eternity* and settled in for a long read.

He knew neither Paul nor Evelyn had gotten a good look at him, but that was no reason to get careless. The chances of them being on the same flight, or even at the airport, were slim, but when boarding began he watched from a safe distance and was the last to board.

"Jesus Christ, why didn't you answer my calls?" Litvak said when Rico finally called.

"I was a little busy."

"Just tell me you got it."

"I didn't—not yet."

"What is 'not yet' supposed to mean?"

Rico retraced his steps from his last conversation with Litvak until his departure from Honolulu. When he reached the part where he killed Rachel, he said, "For a minute I thought I had made a mistake."

"That wouldn't be the first time, would it?"

"Yeah, it would."

"Then, I guess it's good that you got the right one," Litvak said condescendingly. "I wouldn't want you to fuck up for the first time on account of some bad information I fed you."

Rico ignored the remark and finished describing what had taken place.

Litvak sighed heavily. "I don't like this," he said. "I don't like it at all. How come you're so sure you're going to get it back?"

"Jerry and I checked out the lawyer, Paul Elliott—he works at a big firm downtown—and the wife. They're both straight shooters. Solid citizens with good reputations. Went to college together so they knew each other from before. They were in Honolulu at the same time by coincidence and bumped into each other."

"So, what's your point?"

"Jerry got the dope on Elliott from a bailiff at the courthouse who owed me a favor. And he did some nosing around in the woman's neighborhood. They both got deep roots here. They're not gonna skip town with this necklace the way the husband did. They'll be back."

"You're assuming they don't know how much it's worth."

"Maybe they do and maybe they don't. My guess is they do. I'm not saying they won't be tempted, but when push comes to shove they won't do it. The two people I left in Honolulu, yes, but not these two."

"You're pretty damn sure of yourself."

"I know who I'm dealing with. Jerry just confirmed what I already dug up on my own before I hit town. With technology the way it is, it's amazing what you can find out about people in a few minutes these days. You should try it sometime."

"That's what I got you for."

"I know everything there is to know. Believe me, they're coming back."

"You ever see *The Treasure of Sierra Madre?*" Litvak asked.

"Yeah, they call it fiction."

"Then what about the cops? Maybe they're smart enough to figure this out, too."

"So what if they do? The necklace isn't hot and nobody even knows it's missing. The old lady isn't coming back early to check on the condition of these stones."

Chapter Twenty-Eight

The old lady was Katherine Coddington. Her husband Randolph Coddington was an obscenely wealthy businessman. While making his fortune in the silver mining industry in the western United States, he learned something about precious stones. Rubies, although scarcer in this country and of lesser quality, had been found in North and South Carolina...and in Montana, where Coddington's appetite for the gems was first whetted when one of his companies unearthed a few quite by chance. He had been totally oblivious to rubies, but he was immediately taken by their beauty, even in their untreated state.

He immersed himself in their lore, quickly learning where the most precious ones were found and how many of the choicest came from Burma. Through his connections he heard about the necklace as soon as it appeared on the black market in Bangkok in 1955. He purchased it for an unknown sum, then spirited it out of the country.

He gave the necklace to his wife, twenty-five years his junior. She was not nearly as taken with it as he was.

"And what am I to do with this?" she asked.

He had presented it to her with so much excitement that he could barely contain himself.

"I thought you would be as thrilled to receive it as I am to give it to you."

"Randolph, I know you mean well, but this is just another one of your trophies. I'm sure it is as precious and rare as you say, but you know how I feel about such things."

He hung his head a little. "Yes, I know. But this necklace is so special. I thought you might recognize that."

Despite the difference in their ages, she cared for him deeply and she knew that he loved her, but he was not a man who easily showed his emotions. A passionate kiss, a warm embrace—and more of his time. These were the things she longed for but seldom received.

"If you want to do something special for me, surprise me with a dozen roses. Then drop everything and whisk me off to New York for dinner and a Broadway play," she said. "Do that and I'll proudly wear this necklace. And the next day let's go to London, then Paris, Rome, Venice. I've never seen Venice. I'd love to see it with you."

He promised, and he really intended to keep his promise, but he never did take her to any of those places, and she seldom wore the necklace. It lived instead in a safe at the couple's sprawling mansion in Lake Forest, one of Chicago's toniest suburbs.

Mrs. Coddington now lived in the house alone. Her husband had died more than two decades earlier. For years her three grown children and her many grandchildren begged her to move into a smaller place, but she had shrewdly delayed making a decision. She had a live-in housekeeper, and a man who was both landscaper and handyman also lived in a separate cottage on the property. But she was a spry octogenarian, able to take care of her own daily needs without assistance and able to cook her own meals on the occasional nights she wasn't up to eating out or having dinner with one of her children.

Percy Swyte, the handyman, was a recent employee, hired after the sudden death of his predecessor. Since Katherine was in need of a replacement in short order, she performed only a cursory check of his references. Had she taken more time, she would have discovered his criminal record and his addiction to gambling.

Katherine and her three children discussed the ultimate disposition of the necklace frequently. In all the years since her husband had given it to her they had never had it appraised, although its immense value was not in dispute. Everyone generally agreed that for tax reasons it should be sold at auction before her death to avoid becoming part of her estate. She, however, put off making the necessary arrangements just as she had postponed moving. Both the necklace and the house were tangible reminders of the husband she had loved.

One day while unclogging the kitchen sink, Swyte overheard one of these discussions taking place in an adjoining room. Her son remarked that, if the necklace were to continue to languish unseen, it made no sense to keep it in the house safe. He'd feel more comfortable if it were in a safety deposit box.

Swyte, heavily in debt to Litvak, was more than slightly impressed. He devised a scheme to get his hands on the necklace but he needed Litvak, so he told him about the necklace.

"I'd been all over the house but I never seen this safe," he said. "Then it came to me. I'd never been inside any of the closets. No reason to. So I figure it's gotta be in her bedroom closet. I wait until they all go out to dinner and I come in through a window I leave unlocked. Sure enough, there it is, right there in her closet."

"Let me guess," Litvak said. "You can't get in the safe."

"Not only that. From what I heard, this thing is worth a fortune. It's too big for me. I can't unload it."

"But I can," Litvak said. "Tell me some more about it."

* * *

Swyte described the necklace in as much detail as he could based on what he had overheard. It only gave Litvak a vague idea of how much the necklace might be worth, but what he heard made his mouth water. "I know some people," Litvak said. "They can get into the house, knock out the security system, and open the safe without causing any damage. But she's gotta be away for more than just the time it takes to eat dinner."

"She will be. That's why I dropped in on you now," Swyte said. "She's taking a cruise around the world with two of her grandkids. They're leaving in six weeks."

"You've been a busy boy. Can we wait until then?"

"The old lady keeps stalling about the safe deposit box, like everything else. They're supposed to talk about it again when she comes back."

"You sure?"

"Positive."

"How long is this trip gonna last?"

"I thought I heard a couple of months but I wanted to make sure, so I says to the maid, 'Wish I could spend two months gallivantin' around the world like her,' and she says to me it's closer to three."

"Okay. This will square you with me. And after I find out what we're talkin' about, I'll cut you in for a piece of the necklace. But I gotta find out what it's worth first. Meanwhile, you sit tight until you hear from me. And keep your mouth shut."

Swyte did as he was ordered. He sat tight and kept his mouth shut. Little good it did him. The same men Litvak sent to steal the necklace shot and killed him before they left the grounds. When Katherine Coddington discovered that the necklace was missing, Swyte would have been the prime suspect. Alive, he could lead them to Litvak. Dead, he couldn't.

* * *

Litvak continued to dispute Rico's contention that Paul and Evelyn would return to Chicago and that they would bring the necklace with them.

"Okay, maybe—just maybe we don't have to worry about the cops," Litvak said to Rico. "But I still think that if these two people know what this thing is worth, they don't come back."

"It doesn't matter whether they do or don't know. If they don't, there's no reason to leave it behind. If they do, they also know it's why some guy's been chasing them around Honolulu, and they won't get him off their backs by leaving it there. What if he shows up in Chicago looking for it? 'I left it with the police in Honolulu' isn't the response he's looking for. Even if I'm wrong and they're as crooked as the day is long, I know she'll come back to bury her husband—and it wouldn't make any sense to leave the necklace in Hawaii while she's here. They'll be back, with the necklace. Count on it."

Rico was as confident as he led Litvak to believe, with one big exception. What if Paul and Evelyn decided they were safer not carrying the necklace? He couldn't be sure they would *not* leave the necklace with the Honolulu police, or even deliver it to the Chicago police once they got back. It was also possible that Honolulu would insist on holding it as evidence. That concerned him. But there was nothing he could do about it, so he put it out of his mind.

There was one other thing he hadn't been straight with Litvak about. It was true that Jerry had talked to a bailiff who confirmed everything about Paul that was in the public record, and then some. But what he told Litvak about Jerry nosing around Evelyn's neighborhood was a lie.

Sending him to the school to try to find out where she was, was one thing. There were a lot of innocent reasons why someone might want to know that. But actually developing information from neighbors to confirm that she was an upstanding citizen—and doing it without arousing suspicion—was way above Jerry's pay grade. Fortunately, Rico didn't need that additional corroboration. It was solely for Litvak's benefit.

He had asked Jerry to do one other thing that didn't concern Litvak or the necklace. He had tried online and had drawn a blank. He wasn't sure why, but he asked him to check the public records for information about Rachel's family.

Chapter Twenty-Nine

Evelyn made arrangements with the Honolulu authorities to have the bodies returned to Chicago for burial. She had insisted that Rachel's elderly parents let her make arrangements, since she was already doing so for Robert. They were both shaken by their daughter's death and the grisly circumstances surrounding it and would have been ill equipped to attend to things themselves. Rachel's brother hadn't yet arrived from Oregon, where he lived with his family.

Evelyn saw no need to share any of the sordid details with them, so she dissembled prodigiously and didn't regret it.

She didn't know if the police would ultimately tell them about the investigation, but it was fine with her if they didn't. If they chose to, or if the affair were otherwise made public, she would deal with it then. For now, she told family and friends that they had no idea who the murderer was, what his motive was, or why Rachel and Robert had become his victims. Most people accepted her explanations. Rachel's mother, however, was harder to deceive.

"How well did you know my daughter?" she asked during one of her telephone conversations with Evelyn.

"We weren't best friends, Mrs. Gatlin, but we were good friends. I think I knew her pretty well."

"The reason I ask is that I, of course, knew her very well, and it's so hard to believe that she could be murdered like that and that no one would have a clue why."

"It's a mystery to everybody, Mrs. Gatlin."

"What I mean is that while I loved my daughter very much, I know she wasn't perfect. And I know about some of the mistakes she's made. So it would be such a comfort to me to know that…"

"To know what, Mrs. Gatlin?"

"This is very hard for me to say, but I'll come right out and say it. It would be a comfort to me to know that nothing Rachel did caused your husband's death."

Evelyn put her hand over her mouth to keep from gasping into the phone, but she recovered quickly. "Oh no. Of course not. I've heard those rumors, too, and that's just what they are—rumors. There was nothing between Rachel and Robert. I'm sure of it. We were all very good friends. It's a shame that a few people are trying to drag her name—and his—through the mud. Please don't believe them."

"But are you certain, Evelyn?"

"Yes, Mrs. Gatlin. I'm very certain."

"I'm sorry if I've upset you, Evelyn, but I needed to know. I feel so much better now."

"Don't feel sorry. I'm glad I could help."

Through it all, Evelyn put on a brave front, but deep down she was still an emotional wreck. She agreed to spend the night with a favorite aunt in one of the south suburbs instead of in her own apartment. She'd waited until she got back to tell her parents, who were traveling in Europe. They cut their vacation short but wouldn't arrive until the next day. When she finally found herself in bed alone, she cried herself to sleep.

When Paul reached his apartment, he dropped his luggage at the door and immediately Googled a number on his cell. He made reservations for that evening and eight the next morning. Then he went to his bedroom closet and unlocked a small cabinet. He pulled out a .45 automatic pistol, an army issue Beretta 92SB-F—the gun that had won the competition over the Sig Sauer to become the standard handgun for the US military. He checked his watch. He wasn't due at the firing range for a few hours. He lay on his bed, gun in hand, staring at the ceiling. Slowly his eyes closed. He didn't stir until it was time to go.

Chapter Thirty

Attired in a charcoal-gray pinstriped suit, crisp white shirt, and solid gray tie, Paul drove directly from the firing range to Country Club Hills to pick up Evelyn. They'd agreed the day before to go to Litvak's office at ten that morning. Each wanted to go alone, and Evelyn failed to convince him once more that he'd done enough. So they would go together, and if he wasn't in they would wait. If he was gone for the day, they'd come back.

As Paul's GPS homed in on her aunt's address, he spotted her standing on the corner, as they'd arranged. It eliminated the need for an uncomfortable conversation with her aunt about where she was going with the handsome college friend she happened to run into in Hawaii shortly before her husband was murdered there.

Evelyn wore a simple black suit and, despite the occasion, looked as ravishing as usual. "Good morning. How did you sleep?"

"Well. How about you?"

"Me, too," she said.

In fact, neither had slept well.

"How did it go with your aunt?"

"I don't think I could have spent the night in my apartment. She was great."

"I'm glad," Paul said.

They settled into an awkward silence. Paul turned on the radio and they listened to NPR until he parked outside Litvak's office building and shut off the ignition. "All set?"

Evelyn took a deep breath. "Yes, I'm ready."

In the anteroom to Litvak's office sat a pretty, bored, blonde secretary at her desk and a large, muscular bodyguard with a crew cut and bulging biceps in a chair in the corner, reading a magazine. When Paul gave their names, the secretary asked if Litvak was expecting them.

"No," Evelyn answered, to Paul's surprise. Last night they had agreed that he would take the lead. "But I'm sure he'll want to see us. Tell him we're here about a missing necklace."

The secretary, who looked put out, made the call and announced them, repeating what Evelyn said. "Yes, sir," she said and hung up. "Have a seat please. He'll see you in a minute." And to the bodyguard, "Mickey, Mr. Litvak would like to see you."

Mickey went in and emerged thirty seconds later. "I gotta search you," he said.

"You what?" Paul was glad he'd left his Beretta in the glove compartment.

"You want to see him, you get searched."

"What about her?"

"She going in?"

"Yes," Evelyn said defiantly.

"Then she gets searched."

Paul looked at her, concerned. "Why don't you wait out here?"

"No! I'm going in."

"Then, we got a problem," the bodyguard said. He strolled to Litvak's door and stood in front of it, expressionless, with his arms folded over his chest.

Paul looked at him and then at Evelyn. She had no compromise in her expression.

"Oh, I'll do it," the secretary said, exasperated. Without waiting to be asked, she rose from her chair and walked to where Evelyn was standing.

Paul and Evelyn were both glad that she had elected not to wear a wire.

After the bodyguard searched Paul, the secretary escorted them into Litvak's office.

Chapter Thirty-One

Ray Gilbert had been looking for his older brother Archie ever since Rico choked him to death in Jean's apartment. Jerry had done a thorough job of disposing of the body. After carting the trunk out of Jean's apartment, they had punched holes in it and filled it with concrete blocks. It lay undisturbed at the bottom of the Chicago River with a lot of other tough guys who had crossed somebody tougher.

Connecting Rico to Archie was easy. Ray knew about Jean because Archie sang her praises. He also knew she was with him the last day anybody saw him alive. But he didn't know, until he asked around, about Jean's relationship with Rico. The brothers knew Rico's reputation but had never laid eyes on him. Some discreet digging got Ray a description and an address.

That let Jean off the hook. There was no need to rough her up once he had what he was looking for. She might know something but she couldn't have laid a finger on Archie. That had to be Rico.

The trouble was, he'd watched Rico's apartment building for days without sighting him. He'd disappeared right after Archie did, and Ray didn't believe in coincidences. But he was getting antsy. Lucky for Jean, Rico finally came back from wherever he'd been. Ray planned to watch him until he decided whether to wait for more proof or kill him outright.

As Ray sat in his car brooding, he thought of the many close shaves he and Archie had survived. They were both vicious hotheads who would pour sand on a man dying of thirst, but Ray was worse, and somehow it seemed Archie always had his back. Like that time Ray convinced Archie to act as lookout while he held up a liquor store on the spur of the moment, just before closing. The place was deserted save for the short, pudgy matron wearing round, metal-framed spectacles and a tight bun of steel-gray hair.

"I don't want to rush you gentlemen, but we're closing in a couple of minutes," she said from behind the counter. "Can I help you find something?"

They didn't answer. Archie lingered at the door, casually facing the street, while Ray headed straight for her. The woman guessed what was coming. "Oh, shit," she muttered, robotically raising her hands above her head.

Ray waved his Glock toward the cash register. "Hand it over."

She shook her head and glared at him.

"Come on!"

She bit her lower lip, opened the register, and handed him the cash. Ray waved her away with the gun and she took a step to one side. He reached over the counter to make sure the drawer was empty. Then he took two steps back. Just as he turned to leave, Archie looked over his shoulder and saw the woman reaching for something under the counter.

"Get down!" he shouted.

Ray fell to the floor, gripping it with both hands, as the woman hoisted a double-barrel shotgun high in front of her. But before she could aim, a volley of shots rang out, the gun slipped from her hands, and she slumped to the floor, the life seeping from her body like air from a punctured tire. Archie had emptied his .38. Only two of the rounds found their mark, but they were true and Ray was alive.

Then there was the time Ray almost got himself killed by a jealous husband. He and Archie were at a bar sipping beers when a curvy blonde came in and sat at an empty table. Her neckline plunged so low that her breasts screamed for attention, and her blue jeans were so tight they fit like another layer of skin. She also wore a ring on her left ring finger, but no husband was in sight. Ray leered at her from the moment she walked in, and as she glanced around the room her eye caught his. She smiled demurely and he lifted his beer in a silent toast. Without acknowledging the gesture, she turned away, crossed her legs seductively, and trained her eyes on the door. That was all Ray needed. He took another swig, winked at Archie, and sidled over to her table. She was still looking at the door when he got there, but she sensed his presence and he knew it.

"You alone?" he asked.

Without looking up, she placed her left hand, palm-down, on the table in front of him so that her wedding ring was plainly visible.

"I already saw that," he said.

Still not turning to face him she said, with less urgency than circumstances warranted, "My husband is parking the car. He should be here any minute."

"Maybe later then."

"No, that's not possible." Her words said no but her eyes said maybe. Ray flashed a smile she pretended not to see and returned to the bar.

"Nothing doing, huh?" Archie said playfully.

"We'll see." Ray continued his vigil even after the husband walked in seconds later. He was still keeping watch when Archie announced he was going to play cards and disappeared into a back room.

The bar had pinball machines, arcade games, and half a dozen pool tables. After a few drinks the man and his wife went to play pool. Before they did, Ray thought he noticed her steal more than one glance at him.

She was a pretty good player. Each of them won one game and now she was winning the tiebreaker. Even from a distance Ray could see that the husband wasn't dealing with his impending loss gracefully. After studying the table several minutes and not finding a decent shot, he slammed the stick down and marched off to the men's room in a huff.

It was the opening Ray was waiting for. When he reached the table he said, "He's not taking it too well, is he?"

"He'll be okay."

Ray glanced toward the men's room. "So how about later?"

"I told you that's not possible," she said. But she didn't mean it. Ray could tell.

Even though he'd banged the table, the husband had managed not to disturb any of the balls. She walked around the table sizing up her next shot and Ray followed.

"Come on," he said. "We both know where this is going."

"Do we?" she teased.

As Ray stood behind her, she leaned across the table, giving him an unobstructed view of her shapely backside. Seduced by her silent invitation, he reached out to help himself.

"What the fuck!" her husband shouted in Ray's ear. And before he could react, he was in a headlock. Both men were big, but the husband was not nearly as solidly built. Ray freed himself and, with a vengeance, sent the other man flying into a wall, knocking the wind out of him. He was on his knees, gasping for air, when Ray pulled his .45 from his jacket and leveled it. The patrons scattered like cockroaches, some crouching on the floor and others hiding behind furniture. Ray would have pulled the trigger if the woman, sneaking up behind him, hadn't smashed the pool stick across his shoulder. He let out a low groan and the gun dropped to the floor. Instantly the man was on him, pummeling him with both fists. Ray held his throbbing collarbone and sank to the floor.

"Get the gun!" the man shouted. "I'll waste this motherfucker!" But the dim light that prevailed everywhere except directly over the pool tables hampered her search.

"Where is it?"

"You mean this?" Archie said, holding the Glock. He was standing close enough to touch the woman, who was on her hands and knees with her back facing him. Her husband stood ten feet away, hovering over Ray.

"Fuck!" Ray shouted.

Ray tried to get to his feet but couldn't.

"Get the hell out!" Archie ordered, and the couple cautiously took a step. "I said get out!" They trotted a few steps and then broke into a full gallop.

Archie turned to Ray, who'd managed to get to his feet. "You okay?"

"Goddamn it, Archie! You shouldn't have let him go."

"How many people in this fucking joint you figure can pick us out of a line up?" Archie said. It was a rhetorical question and Ray didn't bother answering.

Archie draped Ray's arm around his shoulder and helped him shuffle out the door. He was in extreme pain and his shoulder was never quite the same, but he was alive. Again, thanks to Archie.

Sitting in his car staring at the restaurant. Ray knew he had to make up his mind. He couldn't wait there forever. Absentmindedly, he brought his hand to the top of his right shoulder and massaged it. He double-checked his .45. "To hell with it."

Carrying a folded newspaper under his arm, Ray casually entered the cafe and sat at the counter a few tables from Rico and Jerry. Rico had his back to the wall, facing the door as usual, and Jerry sat across from him with the counter to his left. Ray ordered a roll and coffee and buried his face in the paper, trying to look inconspicuous. He thought he had sat close enough to hear them, but they talked more quietly than he had calculated. He could see them clearly from the corner of his right eye but only caught snatches of their conversation.

Jerry rubbed his eyes vigorously and grasped the bridge of his nose with his thumb and index finger. Ray surmised he suffered from hay fever. Then he saw the ring on Jerry's middle finger. The one Jerry promised Rico he would get rid of. Ray thought it looked like his brother's, but Jerry's hand dropped before he could be sure. Was he wrong about Rico? Was Jerry the man he was looking for? He turned a page and sipped his coffee. *Come on, show it to me again.* But the hand stubbornly remained on Jerry's leg.

Rico stood and quickly approached Ray, who had been so intent on getting a good look at the ring that he had no idea whether Rico had spoken to Jerry before he got up or had done so without warning. Ray stared directly into the paper.

"I left my keys in the car," he called back to Jerry. Then he walked past Ray, who waited for the hand to reappear.

Rico returned in a few moments and they had more coffee. Then Rico noticed the ring. He shook his head. "I thought we talked about this."

"What can I say? I held on to it a little longer than I planned."

"Lose it, Jerry. Today. Not tomorrow."

Jerry looked down at the floor. "You're right. It's as good as done."

"So, did she have any family?" Rico asked.

"Mother and father here and a brother in Oregon." Jerry slid a piece of paper across the table to Rico. "I wrote down the names and addresses."

Rico glanced at it, then folded it and put it in his shirt pocket.

Jerry looked at Rico, sensing something not quite right. "If what Frank said is true, she had it coming. I wouldn't let it bother me."

"It doesn't." And it didn't—much. Rico looked at his watch. A few seconds later he left a tip on the table. On the way to his car he took the paper out of his shirt, unfolded it, and pondered it a long moment before tossing it in a nearby trash can. Jerry stayed another ten minutes finishing a third cup of coffee. Occasionally he raised his left hand to his eyes, but never long enough for Ray to get a good look at the ring. When he finally paid the check and left, Ray was about to follow. But Jerry came back, looking as though he'd forgotten something. He walked past Ray, through the café, and down a flight of stairs over which a sign was posted for restrooms. Ray waited sixty seconds and followed.

In the bathroom he found Jerry standing in front of one of three urinals. He bent down to see whether the one stall in the room was empty, then locked the door behind him and pulled a .45 from his belt. Jerry heard the click of the lock and realized he was in trouble. He turned his head enough to see the gun pointed at his back.

"Hold your dick in your right hand and stick out your left arm so I can see that ring on your finger." Jerry complied. "Where'd you get that?"

"Guy I know gave it to me," Jerry said as calmly as possible. He was still facing the wall.

"Was the guy's name Gilbert?"

"Could've been. Who wants to know?"

"Don't get smart with me or I'll blow your fucking dick off. *I* wanna know."

"I think it was Gilbert. Can I turn around now?"

"No. Wash the piss off that ring so I don't get any of it on me—and use soap. Then get back over here in front of that last pisser and put your hands against the wall." Jerry did as he was told. "Why did he give it to you?" Jerry hesitated. "Think fast."

"He owed me money and let me hold the ring till he paid me back."

"How much money?"

"I don't know, maybe—"

"How much?"

"Maybe a couple of thousand."

"How did he get into you for that much money?"

Jerry tried to stall to buy time. "For Christ sakes, man. What *is* this?"

"I said how?"

"Poker."

"My brother doesn't play poker."

"Maybe it wasn't poker. Maybe I made a mistake. It's a little hard to concentrate right now." Jerry was starting to sweat. "Can we talk about this?"

Ray marched up to Jerry and rammed the .45 into the small of his back. Jerry grunted in pain and doubled over.

"You lying piece of shit. He doesn't play poker or any other card game." He did, but Ray had a hunch. "And he'd never let you hold that ring for a couple thousand dollars. You either tell me the truth or I'm going to blow your fucking brains out."

Jerry grimaced and tried to straighten up. "Okay, okay. I didn't have anything to do with it. A guy I know took him out."

"Why?"

"It was self-defense."

"What do you mean self-defense? Talk to me."

"There was a woman involved. That's all I know. I swear. I just helped myself to the ring. That's the truth—no shit."

"No shit?"

"No shit, man."

"Who's the guy?"

"If I told you that, I'd be as dead as your brother."

"You may be anyway."

"Come on. Gimme a break. You got the ring. This won't bring your brother back."

"Was Rico the guy?"

After a second, Jerry said, "I told you, I can't tell you who the guy was."

"That's okay. You just did."

"Wait a minute! You got it all wrong!"

Ray took two steps toward Jerry until they were only a few feet apart. "Flush it. The stench is killing me."

Warily, Jerry flushed the urinal and, as he did, Ray flushed the other two, sending the roar of rushing water cascading through the room. Jerry knew what was coming. *You lead this life, it catches up with you.* Then he glanced at the ring. *But I brought this one on myself.*

He spun around to make a desperate grab for the gun, but Ray evaded his grasp and buried three bullets in his chest. He staggered backward a few paces until the wall interrupted his momentum. Then he sank to the floor in a squatting position before keeling over on his side. Ray slipped the ring off Jerry's wet finger and calmly left the bathroom unnoticed.

Chapter Thirty-Two

"Please come in," Litvak said from behind his desk. His expensive black suit, gray turtleneck, hefty gold neck chain, and diamond-studded pinky ring made him look every inch the loan shark he was. "I don't believe we've met, Mrs. McDuffie, but I knew your late husband." Evelyn stared at him. He smiled, not at all self-consciously, and turned to Paul. "You must be..."

"Paul Elliott. A friend."

"I see," Litvak said, and motioned to his secretary to leave.

"Excuse me. Could you interrupt us if my office calls? I'm expecting an important message from the courthouse and I told them they could reach me here. I hope that's all right."

"No problem," the secretary said and closed the door.

Litvak smiled broadly. "Did you forget your cell phone, counselor?"

"How did you guess?" Paul said dryly.

The two men sized each other up. Then Litvak said, "Now that that's settled, please." With a sweep of his arm he motioned them to two straight-backed chairs facing him. He leaned in with anticipation, clasping his meaty hands together and resting them on the desk. Paul understood immediately that he had engineered the murders in Honolulu and the dogged attempts to recover the necklace from Evelyn. This was the real thing.

"To what do I owe the pleasure—or should I guess?"

From the moment Paul introduced himself the two men had locked eyes and all but ignored Evelyn. But it was she who answered, with remarkable composure.

"No, we'll tell you." She reached in her purse for the necklace and put it on the desk. "My husband said this belongs to you." She was wound so tightly she felt she might explode, but she had pronounced the words smoothly.

Litvak reached for it, trying mightily to conceal his excitement, caressing it with his eyes. Paul looked at Evelyn. She hid her fear well. He watched Litvak examine the necklace.

"This looks like a nice piece of jewelry. The rubies are pigeon-blood..."

"Pigeon-blood red," Paul said.

"Yes, I thought they might be. But no, it doesn't belong to me."

Paul understood the game and played along. "In that case, if you'll hand it over there's no reason for us to stay."

"What I mean is that *technically* it doesn't belong to me," Litvak said quickly. "I don't know where your late husband laid his hands on it, but he owed me one hell of a lot of money. Nothing in writing, you understand. Just a handshake. I'm sure what he meant was that this would wipe the slate clean, so to speak."

Every word emboldened Evelyn, who said angrily, "It must have been a pretty big slate."

Litvak leaned back in his chair and grinned. "Oh, it was huge."

Although things had not unfolded exactly as Paul and Evelyn had discussed, they had actually ended up where they wanted to be. They had decided that if Litvak would accept the necklace and agree to a truce, despite the perils of that position it was the best they could hope for. They were willing to take their chances that he would keep his word. Paul closed the deal.

"Then we're done," he said in his best lawyer voice. "You go your way and we go ours."

"Why not? We'll call it even."

His last remark provoked an unexpected response from Evelyn. "What do you mean 'call it even'?" She rose from her chair, then glanced balefully at Paul. Her eyes apologized—she knew they hadn't planned it this way. She returned her gaze to Litvak and said with contempt, "You think a piece of jewelry is worth two people's lives?"

"What two people?"

"You know perfectly well," Paul said forcefully.

"Are you accusing me?" Litvak glared at Evelyn.

"Hold on." Paul stood. "I'm accusing you."

"No, *you* hold on! Who do you think you're talking to?"

"Someone who has to have people searched before they come into his office," Evelyn said, her voice quavering a little.

"They search people before they come into the courthouse, don't they, counselor?"

"And prisons, too," Paul said.

"This is my property and I do what I want on my own property."

Evelyn should have stopped, but did not. "Does that include having people killed?"

Agitated, Litvak leaped up from his desk and charged her like a bull. She fell back in alarm as Paul blocked his path. Though a few inches taller, Paul didn't have his girth. But he stood his ground and stopped Litvak, surprised by his audacity, just short of her. Litvak leaned around Paul to make eye contact with her. "Who told you I had these people killed? Where's your proof? If what you say is true, why haven't the police arrested me?"

"We didn't come here to spar with you," Paul said. "You've heard our proposition. Do we have a deal?"

Litvak wasn't about to be patronized by some smart-ass, big-shot lawyer. "You accuse me of doing murder and you don't want to 'spar' with me about it? Well I want to spar with you about it." His voice rose with righteous indignation. "I'll tell you another thing," he said, jabbing his finger at Paul. "Bobby was a two-bit hustler who didn't pay his debts. I gave him a break and he stabbed me in the back. And you can bet I wasn't the only one he stiffed. Go find those poor sons of bitches, because maybe one of them returned the favor. But not me. I don't have people killed." He smiled serenely. Strangely, his speech had a calming effect on him.

But Evelyn exploded. "I hate your guts and your pious attitude. I wish I had the stomach to hire someone to kill you the way you killed them!"

"My, my, my," Litvak said dismissively, folding his arms across his chest. He hesitated a moment, feigning deep thought. "Okay, I'll keep the necklace because I'll never see the money he owed me." Then he raised the ante. He put his hands in his pockets and grinned malevolently. "By the way, Mrs. McDuffie, I don't know why you're so bent out of shape. After all, Bobby *was* banging your girlfriend, wasn't he?"

Evelyn lost what little self-control she had left. Paul still partially separated them, but she was close enough. She drew back her hand and slapped Litvak hard across the face. He flushed and lunged for her with both arms. Suddenly Paul was back in his old neighborhood. He instinctively blocked Litvak, pivoted, and caught him with a vicious elbow to the nose. Litvak fell back hard against his desk and groaned, blood spurting from his nose.

"Goddamn it! Mickey, get in here!"

Mickey rushed into the office. He stopped short and stared at the oozing blood Litvak tried to stanch with a handkerchief. He turned to Paul, who appeared calm and collected but felt seized with dread as he pictured himself in a life-and-death struggle with the muscle-bound bodyguard. Somehow Paul was able to say firmly, "Did the judge call? I didn't hear the phone." That got Mickey's attention. He hesitated and looked to Litvak for guidance.

Litvak raised his head slightly and, holding the handkerchief in place with one hand, made a fist with his free hand and pounded the top of the desk. "Get the fuck out of here—now!"

They left quickly without a word but didn't rush. But when they were safely outside, Paul put his arm around Evelyn's waist and swept her along with him as he walked briskly to the car. She glanced behind her to make sure Litvak hadn't changed his mind and unleashed

Mickey. The thought had crossed Paul's mind, too. Once inside the car he reached past Evelyn to open the glove compartment, removed his .45, and placed it in his lap. They sped away, all the while keeping a lookout behind them.

A few hundred yards down the street Paul felt able to breathe for the first time since they left Litvak's office, and some of the tension that still gripped his body slowly started to ebb. "Needless to say, that didn't exactly go as planned."

When Evelyn didn't respond, he looked over and saw her trembling. He pulled over and turned off the engine. Her hands were clasped tightly in her lap, her shoulders were hunched, and she stared blankly ahead. He took her shoulders and gently turned her toward him. She lowered her eyes but he bent his head until his eyes met hers. "Hey, it's all over," he said softly.

She took several deep breaths to try to regain her composure. "I'm sorry. I could've gotten us both killed."

"You think so?" Paul said, trying to coax a smile out of her.

She didn't quite manage one. "Thanks." It was not much above a whisper.

"I didn't know you were such a tiger."

"I'm not. He was so smug and insufferable that I...I just lost my temper."

"That makes two of us."

"I wish I could take it back."

"Don't worry." Paul started the car and pulled back into traffic.

"You surprised me," Evelyn said after a few blocks. "You're always so..."

"In control?"

"Exactly. How did you know what I was thinking?"

"I'm a good guesser."

"In all the years we've known each other I've never seen you lose your temper."

"You found me out."

"No, seriously, Paul. Even back there with Litvak I'm not sure you really lost it. Your reaction was—I don't know—calculated."

"Mostly it was reflexes."

"Mostly?"

"Yes."

"Then you admit there was some calculation involved."

"Yes."

"You're a strange guy, Paul. Nice, but strange."

"Is that a compliment?"

"I thought you were a good guesser." They drove a few more miles in silence. "What do you think will happen now?"

"We took a gamble. We gave him what he wanted. Now we'll just have to see if that's all he wanted."

"What about what just happened?"

"Your slap or my elbow?" Paul said.

"Both."

"He's a big boy. He'll get over it." But he wasn't as sure as he sounded. Litvak was clearly full of himself and had undoubtedly had his pride wounded. That could spell trouble. But they'd done the best they could under the circumstances.

"I hope so," Evelyn said.

They arrived at Evelyn's aunt's house and Paul parked down the block. "How about dinner?"

"That'd be nice. I'll have to sneak away from relatives and friends, but I'm sure I can."

They chose a little French restaurant in the Hyde Park neighborhood. "I'd better meet you there," Evelyn said. "How about 7:30?"

"See you then."

As he drove away, Paul wondered how long they would have to wait to find out if Litvak had decided to back off. And if he decided not to, maybe he would send Mickey or someone like him to deliver the message. If so, he wondered what chance they had to survive.

Chapter Thirty-Three

From the airport Rico had gone directly to Jean's apartment, and they made love as though they'd been apart for months. If the lingering tension between them didn't melt away entirely, it receded far into the background. They lost themselves in each other's embrace.

The next day Rico drove to his apartment, unpacked, and met Jerry for coffee. Then he returned to Jean's apartment. Their time together the night before had not quenched their pent-up desire. They made wondrous love, and afterward took a long, relaxing shower together. He got out first, leaving her behind to shampoo her hair. As he dried off, he heard his cell phone and he went out to the living room to answer it.

"Hey, did you hear about Jerry?" Litvak asked.

"No, what?"

"Somebody popped him. In the john at that dump near your place. The coffee shop."

Rico had known Jerry a long time. He was the closest thing he had to a best friend—any close friend, really. They never talked about getting killed, but they both knew it could happen. Maybe it shouldn't have come as a shock, but it did.

"Shit, I was just there with him a few hours ago. When did it happen?"

"Must've been right after you left. Some guy pumped three slugs in his chest and walked away. Nobody even saw the guy. Any of this make sense to you?"

He felt bad for Jerry, but his next thought was self-preservation. Whoever wanted to get rid of Jerry might want him out of the way, too. He got a sick feeling in the pit of his stomach. "I'm not sure—did they lift anything off him?"

"He had his wallet and some cash. And he had his watch, but that wasn't worth shit."

"What about a ring?"

"I never knew Jerry to wear a ring."

"He picked one up a little while ago—a good one."

"Hold on a minute." Litvak came back on the line after a few seconds. "I just talked to somebody who was there. No ring on him."

"Fuck."

"What's that supposed to mean?"

"I may know who did him."

"Who?"

"I don't know the guy's name, but if it was him, it's personal."

Jean emerged from the bathroom. One towel was wrapped around her torso and another around her hair. She sat on the couch near Rico and began drying her hair with the towel.

"I feel for Jerry. We'll lay him out real good, but if it's personal, it's personal. I still got a piece of business to deal with," Litvak said.

Rico meandered to the other side of the room out of earshot from Jean. "You talked to the woman?"

"Yeah, I did."

"And?"

"They left the necklace."

"So now you're straight."

"Not quite. I don't trust them to put this thing behind them."

"Why not?"

"They both got way out of line. The bitch started it, and before I knew it the guy surprised me and caught me with a lucky elbow in the nose. I think the black motherfucker broke it."

Rico smiled to himself. "The lawyer did that?"

"Nobody breaks my nose and walks."

"And where was Mickey while all this was going down?"

"Fuck Mickey."

"So now it's personal—like with Jerry?"

"You're goddamned right it's personal," Litvak said.

"What if the cops know they came to see you?"

"The cops can kiss my ass. Lots of people come to see me. I don't even care if they told the cops they left it here. If the cops can find a necklace in this joint, they must be Houdini."

"You sure about this?"

"You're asking that question a lot these days."

"You noticed."

"What're you poppin' off about? If you hadn't lost the damn thing in the first place, none of this would be happening. So just clean up your own mess and don't be such a smart ass. I want 'em dead."

"That's the wrong way to go on this."

"I didn't ask your opinion."

"You didn't have to."

"Listen, I put up with your shit long enough. It's about time you learned who's running things around here. Now this is what's gonna happen. Either you get rid of these two people, or I have somebody pay that girlfriend of yours a visit. I guarantee you won't recognize the body. And don't bother asking who's gonna do the job. She won't see it coming and you won't either. And one more thing. That job gets done even if something happens to me. I don't think you have the balls, but why take chances? Enough said?"

"That would be a mistake."

"I don't think so. See, I threaten *you*, you don't give a shit, because you're Mr. Tough Guy. You think nobody can take you out. But I say *she* gets it, it's a different story because you don't know who, you don't know when, and you don't know how."

"I was you, I wouldn't bring her into this."

"You ain't me and I just did."

With that, Litvak disconnected.

* * *

Rico went over to the window and stared out, deep in thought. From as far back as he could remember, he had always been a loner, had always done things his way—without any help if he could. His father worked in the steel mill and his mother worked as a maid in a hotel. He had an older brother and sister and two younger brothers. The year he started kindergarten, his older siblings would be attending a different school. That created a problem for his parents because there were no school buses in his town, which meant Rico would have to walk to school alone, a distance of about a mile through streets that were unfamiliar to a five-year-old. His father would be able to take him when he was working either the four-to-twelve shift or the night shift, but he couldn't take him when he was working the day shift, as was true on the first day of school. His grandmother couldn't take him because she was tied up watching his two younger brothers, one of whom was an infant, and of course his mother couldn't take him because she worked during the day.

His mother solved the problem by asking a neighbor, Mrs. Hollingsworth, who also had a son in kindergarten, to allow Rico to walk to and from school with them. The plan worked fine on the way to school, but after school Rico eluded Mrs. Hollingsworth, found an alternate way home, and was waiting there for her when she arrived, anxious and worried. When his parents asked why he hadn't waited, he said simply that he knew the way home—a shorter one at that—and didn't need Mrs. Hollingsworth to show him. The next day—and every day after that—he walked to school alone.

Rico was a smart kid but never applied himself in school. He knew college wasn't for him, so what was the point? Still, he was a voracious reader because he liked words and he liked ideas. His tastes ran mostly to historical fiction and crime novels. Nobody knew about that side of him, though, except the school librarians. He didn't care what the tough guys in the neighborhood might think or say, although no one would have been bold enough to say a word, but his parents might wonder why someone who read so much did so poorly in school, and he didn't want to have that conversation. So he did his reading alone in his bedroom with the door closed when nobody was around.

His mother died when he was ten. She'd had a hard life and one day her heart just stopped. The official cause was congestive heart failure aggravated by diabetes. She was only forty-nine. There was a special bond between Rico and his father, but all of it was internalized and words of affection never passed between them. When he was sixteen his father was diagnosed with terminal pancreatic cancer. By then his older brothers and sisters had moved out.

Everyone assumed Rico's father committed suicide, and in a way, he did. After the cancer had ravaged his body, he was just waiting to die at home. Early one morning he finally summoned the courage to put a gun to his head, but he couldn't pull the trigger. He begged Rico to do it and Rico stoically obliged, but later that night alone in the house he cried. It was the last time he ever did.

He had handled his father's agony alone. He had to deal with this new development alone, too. And he would. He could justify killing the other woman, but this one was innocent. And he admired the lawyer for standing up to Litvak.

But now Jean was involved. That was a problem. And it wouldn't go away.

"I thought you said everything was okay," Jean said from the couch.

"It is," Rico said, as though coming out of a trance.

Jean was encouraged by Rico unexpectedly opening up to her earlier, so she plowed ahead. "Do you want to tell me about it?"

"No."

"Goddamn you, Rico. I can tell something is bothering you. When something is bothering me, I talk to you about it, but you never open up about anything."

He faced her. "Haven't we had this discussion before?"

"Rico, we don't discuss anything. You talk and I listen."

"That's just the way it has to be sometimes."

"Sometimes?"

"Okay, most of the time."

"Like the other day when you almost sliced my face up?"

"We back to that again? I said I was sorry."

"How could you say it was just business?"

"Because it was."

Tired of banging her head against a wall, Jean stood and joined him at the window. "I give up."

"It's who I am, Jean. From day one I never tried to hide that from you."

"I know, but there's more to you than what you do. You said so yourself. If there wasn't, do you think I could be with you now after what you did? I see something in you that you don't even see in yourself."

"You see what you want to see, but I am who I am."

"And why are you here with me?"

"Because we understand each other."

"Sometimes I think you do understand me, Rico, maybe even more than I understand myself. But I don't think I'll ever understand you. I don't think anybody does."

"One out of two ain't bad."

"I'm serious, Rico. Don't you ever stop to think about the consequences of what you do?"

He looked serious. "I do a job or I don't. If I do it, I do it and it's over."

"And what happens when you don't do it?"

"The same thing that happens when you see a john and something about him doesn't feel right. I walk away." He looked directly in her eyes. "But Jean, that doesn't happen every day—and it's not happening today."

His eyes were cold and distant. She lowered her gaze and slowly walked back to the sofa. Without a word Rico strode past her and went into the bedroom to get dressed.

Chapter Thirty-Four

Rico was parked across the street from Paul's apartment building when he drove up. Getting in and out wouldn't be easy. There was a doorman and a security door and plenty of foot traffic. He resolved to wait. Paul didn't emerge again until seven. No way to get to him before he reached his car. Rico followed.

And Ray followed Rico. He saw that Rico was trailing the man who lived in the apartment building. Ray had no idea who he was and he didn't care. If Rico was following someone, he'd be concentrating on him and not on who might be following him. Maybe this would be the night.

Paul had no trouble finding a place to park on the street. Business was moderate on a weeknight. Inside the hostess showed him to a table near the front of the restaurant. He faced the door so he could see Evelyn when she came in.

The restaurant was on a quiet, tree-lined street. The decor was pleasant, the portions generous, and the food exquisite. The intimate rectangular dining room accommodated only ten tables, four of which were occupied when Paul came in.

Like a lot of lawyers, he was a compulsive reader, and he'd brought a *New Yorker* in case Evelyn was late. He'd only read a few paragraphs when Rico walked in, dressed in a light gray suit and a blue striped shirt with an open collar that revealed a tastefully thin gold neck chain. Paul noticed that he couldn't hear the door as it opened, but it made a distinctive sound when it closed. As it closed behind Rico, he looked up from his magazine long enough to see it wasn't Evelyn and continued reading.

Like Wild Bill Hickok was rumored to do, Rico always sat facing the door, but he asked the hostess to seat him at a table with a clear view of Paul. Of the tables that weren't occupied, the only one that fit that description required him to sit with his back to the door. He hesitated, then took a seat. Only a few tables separated them. Paul had to look directly over Rico's left shoulder to see the door. It opened and closed a few times as people came and went, causing him to look up from his magazine, and Paul found himself, between glances, staring at Rico as he perused his menu. Something about Rico was ominous and unsettling and... vaguely familiar. Paul couldn't put his finger on it.

Rico could feel Paul's eyes intermittently coming to rest on him like a stone skipping across the surface of a pond in slow motion, but he was careful not to let him know, making sure that he slowly put the menu aside before casually raising his eyes and looking past Paul at an unimpressive painting on the wall behind him. When Rico was finished with the menu, Paul quickly averted his eyes and was sure that Rico had not noticed. Seconds later Rico glanced over his shoulder when he heard the door close. Evelyn breezed in, looking more radiant than ever. Paul rose immediately, got her attention with a wave of his hand, and waited for her to join him.

Evelyn joining Paul was a bonus. Rico couldn't be sure when he would find them together again, or whether the circumstances would be right. They had arrived separately and maybe would leave the same way, which might make it difficult to catch them both outside. It looked like it was now or never.

Paul pulled Evelyn's chair out for her. "You look..." He had started to say "stunning" but thought the word too revealing. "You look very nice."

"Thank you," she said, smiling sufficiently to acknowledge the compliment. She wore a cute black dress that matched Paul's herringbone sport coat. "Been waiting long?"

"A few minutes. Did you have a rough afternoon?"

"Yes. We talked about the funeral arrangements. I know it sounds terrible, but it's such a relief to get away."

"No, it sounds natural."

A waiter took their drink order.

After the waiter goes in the kitchen will be as good a time as any, Rico thought.

Paul rose, excusing himself to go to the men's room. Rico tracked his movement out of the corner of his eye for as long as he could, then looked furtively over his left shoulder in time to see where Paul went. He could wait.

Paul washed his hands, straightened his tie and, thinking of Evelyn, gazed at his image in the mirror. *Which is right?* he asked himself. *All good things come to those who wait or he who waits is lost?* He asked himself that all the time, and the unsatisfying answer was always the same: It depends. Okay, but which was the answer now?

After losing Evelyn to Robert in college, he had waited and JoAnne had come into his life. He didn't think he could live without her, but after she was taken away from him, he had waited again and, whether by chance or providence, he had reconnected with Evelyn. Despite enormous intervening tragedy, all good things had come to him. If he waited any longer, would he be lost?

Paul pulled on the door but stopped midway. Something was out of place. Through the partially open door he saw a man in profile standing inside the restaurant vestibule. As his eyes surveyed the man from head to foot, he noticed that the man was propping the front door open with his foot. A voice inside Paul's head told him to wait. *All good things come to those who wait.* He held his breath and didn't move.

Ray had sat in his car, wavering between waiting to waylay Rico when he came out and going in after him. He was still wary of his prey, so the former seemed preferable. But in the end, he sucked it up. He would get it over with. He would have the element of surprise and, if he was lucky, a stationary target in a brightly lit room. He knew the restaurant well. He could enter unnoticed if he kept the door from shutting automatically and silently guided it closed. His foot was in place to do just that when Paul started his abbreviated exit.

Paul didn't see a weapon, but the man looked suspicious and uneasy. He knitted his brow. *Does this answer the question whether Litvak had decided to back off? Was this a message from him?* Paul removed the Beretta from his jacket, held it by his side, and gingerly stepped in front of the bathroom door, using his back to keep it from closing. The man was only a few yards away and, with little effort, would see Paul if he turned his head slightly left.

But Ray focused all his attention directly ahead of him. His right arm had been shielded from Paul's view, but now he raised it purposefully. The slowly ascending hand was holding a pistol. The man was clearly facing Evelyn and was about to take aim at her and fire.

Ray had a clear shot at Rico from the door and, rather than risk getting any closer, he elected to take it. Paul raised his weapon and pointed it with both hands at the man's torso. It would be a tough shot because only his side was exposed. The man grasped his weapon with both hands and trained it in Evelyn's direction,

At that moment Rico felt a chill, the kind he sometimes felt when he was in a tight spot with no apparent way out. Was it his impending death? Then it faded. But there was something more. The words he had spoken to Jean came back to him: "So far I never shot anyone who didn't have it coming." *So far? Was this the end of the string or did these two also have it coming? Did they really?* He started to stand and the same chill gripped his body.

He who waits is lost. Paul tried to draw the man's attention before he fired. "Hey!"

He was too late. Ray managed to squeeze off a shot an instant before Paul's warning shout reached his ears. Then, reacting to Paul's voice, he dropped to one knee and turned left, still gripping the gun with both hands. Paul lowered his arm and, tracking Ray's descent and pivot, rapidly fired four times. Ray got off one shot before the gun dropped from his hands, and he crumpled to the floor in a heap, a look of profound surprise frozen on his face. All four shots had found their mark, three entering the chest and abdomen and one lodging in the left elbow.

Paul rushed into the dining room, clutching the .45 in both hands. His eyes darted from the body on the floor to his and Evelyn's table. *Where is she?* When he looked back at the body a second time, Rico was hovering over it. *Where did he come from?* His and Rico's eyes met, and he remembered that he'd been sitting a few tables away.

"Did you see the woman I was with?" he asked anxiously, his voice filled with alarm.

"She's okay. She hit the floor when the shooting started."

"Thank God! Is he dead?"

"Very." Rico looked at the ring on Ray's finger. It was the same one. The body lay face down, spread eagled on the floor. Rico removed Ray's wallet from his left back pocket. He opened it, located a driver's license, and focused on the photo. "His brother," he said out loud.

"What?" Paul asked.

"Nothing." Rico had made a mental note of Archie's driver's license in Jean's apartment so he could check him out when he got back from Hawaii—to see if he had to worry about someone like Ray. Obviously, he did, and so did Jerry.

All of a sudden Paul's .45 felt extremely heavy, as though someone had tied a dumbbell to his wrist. He put it on a nearby table.

Evelyn got to her feet and searched the room for Paul. He spotted her amidst the pandemonium that engulfed the restaurant and they rushed to each other and embraced.

Something caused Paul to look back at Rico, who now stood facing him. When their eyes met again, Paul knew. Rico put his hands on his hips, parting his jacket slightly and revealing the butt of his Sig Sauer in its blue shoulder holster. Paul remembered that he had left his gun on one of the tables. He shifted his eyes from side to side, searching. It lay roughly mid-way between them. Their eyes met once more.

Rico advanced, stopping a few feet away. "Who was he?" Paul said, managing to keep his galloping emotions in check.

"A guy who wanted to even a score…with me."

"With you?"

"That's right."

"And who are you?"

"A guy whose chestnuts you just pulled out of the fire."

"That's it?"

Rico took his sunglasses from his jacket and put them on. Evelyn brought her hand to her mouth. "Yeah, that's it," he said.

"What about Litvak?"

"Nothing about him."

"So you're saying it's all over—everything?"

"Yes."

"Just like that?"

"Yes."

"Why should we believe you?" Evelyn asked unsteadily.

"Believe what you want," Rico said with utter indifference. Then he walked to the table where Paul had left his gun and returned it to him. "You forgot this." He started for the door.

"What about Honolulu?" Paul said to the retreating back.

"I hear it's a nice place to visit," Rico said, without looking back or slowing his pace.

"I think you should wait for the police."

"I don't."

When he reached the door, Paul pointed his weapon at his back. "Wait!" But Rico didn't wait. He kept walking. Paul lowered his .45 to his side and turned to Evelyn. He had had no intention of trying to stop Rico and Rico knew it.

"Paul, are you all right?" Evelyn asked.

"Yes, I'm fine," he said, but he really wasn't.

"So it was you who...who shot the other man?"

"I thought he was aiming at you."

"Oh, Paul! I'm so sorry."

"It's okay. Really, I'm fine. I'm glad you're all right."

"Have you ever...?"

"No."

"You must feel awful."

"I've felt better. Fortunately, he was no saint. A least I hope he wasn't."

She waited a moment. "Paul, you know that was the man in Honolulu."

"Yes."

"Do you believe him?"

"I don't know about Litvak, but I don't think we have to worry about him. If he had wanted to, he could have killed us both a minute ago." When Paul set the gun down again, Evelyn noticed something on his right hand.

"My God, Paul! You've been wounded."

Paul examined the blood on his hand and then the .45. "No. It came from the gun. It must be his blood." He looked at the floor and saw a trail of blood droplets going out the door.

"Maybe I didn't save his life after all."

Chapter Thirty-Five

As Rico drove away he heard blaring sirens from approaching police cars. He applied pressure to his wound with a handkerchief and gritted his teeth, but he had to smile despite the pain. The same man who'd killed Jerry, and who'd come that close to punching Rico's ticket, was dead. And Rico had had nothing to do with it. The lawyer, of all people! He called Litvak on his Bluetooth. "I need to talk to you tonight."

"Go ahead. I'm listening."

"I mean in person. I don't want to talk about it over the phone."

"Can't this wait?"

"No."

"Meet me at 73rd and South Shore in an hour."

* * *

When Litvak pulled up to the intersection, Rico was waiting. He walked out of the shadows, got in, and settled into the front seat across from Litvak. From the interior light when the door was opened, he could see that Litvak's nose and cheek were bruised. The light was on for only a second and after the door closed, it was dark inside and both men looked straight ahead.

"What's this all about?"

"It's over, Frank. Elliott just saved my life."

"The goddamned lawyer? What do you mean he just saved your life?"

"The guy who nailed Jerry was about to do me when Elliott put four in him."

"Four? Who *is* this guy?"

"He thought he was protecting the woman. But the point is, if he doesn't waste this guy I'm not sitting here talking to you now."

"What kind of bullshit is this? You're telling me you owe this guy because he *accidentally* saved your ass?"

Rico sighed audibly. "That's what I'm telling you."

The finality in Rico's voice worried Litvak, but he still had his ace in the hole. He decided to save it for now. "We already had this conversation, but I don't see what the big deal is," he said, adopting a conciliatory tone.

"A guy saves my life, I don't take him out."

"Okay. The circumstances changed since we talked. I get that. I don't like it but I see your point of view. So what if I decide to be a nice guy and find somebody else to take care of this? That is, as long as you understand this is my decision, not yours."

"I said it's over."

Despite himself, Litvak couldn't contain his rage. "What the fuck's gotten into you? This is my ass—and yours, too."

"It's nobody's ass. This isn't business. It's personal because you got slapped around a little."

Litvak pounded his fist against the dashboard. "Goddamn it, Rico. Are you ordering me not to do this? Because if you are, you just walked right up to the fucking line."

"You're wrong, Frank. Seems to me I stepped all the way over it."

The color drained from Litvak's face, and his bluster evaporated. He and Rico had had their differences, but Rico had never defied him so directly and that worried him. It worried him a lot because Rico had to know that Jean's life was on the line. He gave Rico more leeway than he gave anybody else who worked for him because Rico always got the job done, and he got it done better than anyone else. True, sometimes if he didn't like the setup, he insisted on doing things his way. Litvak didn't like that independent streak but he tolerated it because Rico got results.

And, of course, on top of everything else, beneath his cool exterior Rico was terrifying. Litvak had never known any two men to go up against him and walk away, and when Rico made up his mind about something, it didn't matter what the consequences of the decision were, for him or anybody else. He had already calculated them.

The dressing-down Litvak had administered to Rico over the phone, punctuated with the threat against Jean, had been meant to rein him in. Apparently, it hadn't worked.

So on a cool night Litvak was sweating bullets, because it sounded like Rico had made up his mind about Paul and Evelyn and the consequences be damned. Didn't he know, Litvak mused, that Jean was as good as dead? He turned to him and played his ace. "You know me well enough to know I wasn't bluffing about your girlfriend."

Rico didn't answer and continued facing forward.

"And you know I'm not stupid enough to meet you out here without some insurance. I'd say Mickey should be at your girlfriend's place about now, waiting to hear from me. If I go, she goes. You want me to call him?"

Rico turned to face him. "Call him if you want. I never seen a dead man answer a phone yet." Litvak blanched. "I figured it was Mickey but when I went to his place, I wasn't sure. When I looked in his eyes, I was ninety-nine point nine percent sure. But point one percent is still point one percent. I'm glad I didn't take him out for nothing."

When he made the call to Litvak, Rico had been parked outside Mickey's apartment building. He was almost certain that Litvak had given the job to Mickey because he was the obvious choice to go after Jean. In fact, he was so obviously Litvak's first choice that Litvak counted on Rico ruling Mickey out precisely for that reason. Now all Rico had to do was wait.

He didn't know whether Mickey was headed for Jean's apartment or to rendezvous with Litvak. It didn't matter. Either way, he wasn't going to make it. As he walked to his car on a deserted street, Rico approached him from behind, Sig at his side, and waited for Mickey to sense his presence and react. Hearing Rico's unguarded footsteps, Mickey reached in his coat pocket and, without removing it, grasped his own .45 and turned, expecting the worst. Seeing Rico, his eyes widened as Rico's narrowed, and his heart felt as though it would leap from his chest. He jerked the .45 out of his pocket, but before he could aim, Rico shot him once in the throat and twice in the heart.

Increasingly anxious, Litvak tried to negotiate. "Okay, so I was sending Mickey, but nobody got hurt."

"Because I got to him first. You don't bluff, remember?"

"Listen, we can work something out."

Rico didn't answer.

"You convinced me, okay? You win. You feel that way about it, they walk, okay?"

Rico turned away.

Desperate, Litvak tried again. "You gonna answer me here?" By now his eyes had adjusted to the darkness.

Rico turned to face him once more. "The minute Elliott took that guy out I said to myself, 'That tears it with Frank because no way do I pop this guy now.' I just wanted to tell you to your face. So I told you. Not one word either one of us has said after that makes a bit of difference, and we both know it. You mixing Jean up in this just made it worse. Like I told you, that was a mistake. You made it and Mickey paid for it. You can't let me leave this car alive, and I can't let you. So we might as well get it over with."

Litvak started to raise his left arm. "Wait a—" He didn't finish the sentence. Rico shot him once through the forehead. He never even saw the gun.

Rico turned on the interior light and rolled the body toward him. He knew what he would find but he figured he might as well confirm it: Litvak was still clutching a .45 Glock in his left hand. He made sure he hadn't left any of his blood in the car, wiped his fingerprints off the door handles, and melted into the night. His next stop was the safe in Litvak's office.

* * *

Later that night Rico rang the buzzer downstairs at Jean's apartment building. When she opened the door, she could barely contain her excitement. "Rico, I've been reading your book ever since you left. I really like it." He'd left his copy of *From Here to Eternity* in her apartment.

"Good," Rico said, a little surprised.

"Why didn't you mention it before?"

"I guess I didn't think you'd like it."

"Well, I do. And I think I know why you do."

"Oh?"

"Yes, the main character, Corporal Pruitt—" She saw the blood stain on his side. "My goodness! What happened?"

"It's not serious."

Jean had been so excited to uncover a new layer of Rico's personality that she had neglected to let him out of the doorway. "Come in, come in!" She led him to the sofa.

"You got any peroxide and bandages?" he said, lying down.

"If not, I can get some from the drug store. You sure it's not serious?"

"I'm fine. It went clean through. As a matter of fact, let's go for a drive tomorrow."

She looked at him and smiled. "Whatever you say."

That reminded him. "Somebody took Jerry out today," he said evenly.

"Oh, no! He was always so sweet to me."

"Yeah, he liked you a lot."

"Do the police...?"

"It's already been taken care of."

"Did you...?"

"No, I didn't. By the way, when I left here, I thought I had made up my mind on that piece of business, but I hadn't. Then something made it up for me. I think it worked out okay."

"Good," Jean said and softly kissed him.

Rico returned the kiss and gave her a wistful smile. "Didn't you say you like rubies?"

* * *

Paul and Evelyn went to the police station after the shooting but were unable to identify Rico. The police showed them mug shots, but unenthusiastically. As far as they were concerned, Rico was just an innocent bystander. If he truly was involved in the Honolulu murders, that was a matter for that city's police department.

Each discovered Litvak's death in the morning paper. They met for breakfast and sat in a booth in a secluded corner of the restaurant.

"Who do you think killed him?" Evelyn asked.

"I can only guess."

"You have a pretty good idea, though."

"I feel terrible about what happened to Robert and Rachel. It was a heinous crime, and I couldn't condone it in a million years. But as much as I hate to say it, I think we owe our lives to this man. We'll never know, but I don't believe he had to kill Litvak. Although he probably came here to kill you or me or both of us last night, in the end I think he killed Litvak to protect us."

"Paul, you say you can't condone what he's done, but it sounds like what you're doing."

"No, I'm not—not even for a second."

"Then what? Are you saying that, despite everything, some part of you admires him?"

"No, I don't think so."

"You don't *think* so?"

"I know how it sounds, but I can't help thinking that he saved our lives."

"After he tried to kill us in Honolulu?"

"We don't know that."

"Well, he certainly killed Robert and Rachel. And what about last night? You said it yourself. Why was he at the restaurant if not to kill us?"

She had worn him down.

"Of course, you're right," he said, trying to concede the point and hoping he had succeeded. As good a lawyer as he was, he realized he was never going to make her understand because, in truth, he wasn't sure he did himself.

Evelyn sensed that he hadn't fully acquiesced. "Paul, you really shouldn't."

"Shouldn't what?"

"Admire him—even a little."

"Believe me, Evelyn, I don't."

But he did—a little. And she knew it.

She scooted next to him, put her arms around his waist, and drew him close to her. Then she surprised him. "It's okay if you admire him, but only a little. I'll allow you that much. But you, sir, have my full and undying admiration for taking such good care of me, for protecting me, and for making me feel like a woman for the first time since I can remember."

And she leaned in to kiss him.

THE END

Dear reader,
We hope you enjoyed reading *Pigeon-Blood Red*. Please take a moment to leave a review, even if it's a short one. Your opinion is important to us.

Discover more books by Ed Duncan at
https://www.nextchapter.pub/authors/author-ed-duncan

Want to know when one of our books is free or discounted? Join the newsletter at http://eepurl.com/bqqB3H

Best regards,
Ed Duncan and the Next Chapter Team

About the Author

Ed is a graduate of Oberlin College and Northwestern University Law School. He was a partner at a national law firm in Cleveland, Ohio, for many years. He is the original author of a highly regarded legal treatise entitled *Ohio Insurance Coverage*, for which he provided annual editions from 2008 through 2012. Ed, originally from Gary, Indiana, lives outside Cleveland. He is at work on the second installment in the trilogy that began with *Pigeon-Blood Red*.

Pigeon-Blood Red
ISBN: 978-4-86750-082-8

Published by
Next Chapter
1-60-20 Minami-Otsuka
170-0005 Toshima-Ku, Tokyo
+818035793528
7th June 2021

CPSIA information can be obtained
at www.ICGtesting.com
Printed in the USA
LVHW051021020422
714752LV00003BA/10